the art of *Sleepy Hollow*

Including the screenplay by
ANDREW KEVIN WALKER

With an introduction by
TIM BURTON

Pocket Books
New York London Toronto
Sydney Singapore

POCKET BOOKS, a division of Simon & Schuster, Inc.
1230 Avenue of the Americas, New York, NY 10020

Copyright © 1999 by Paramount Pictures and Mandalay Pictures, LLC.

Design concept by B.L.T. Associates, Inc.
Book design by Joel Avirom, Jason Snyder, and Meghan Day Healey

ISBN: 0-671-03657-2

First Pocket Books hardcover printing November 1999

10 9 8 7 6 5 4 3 2 1

The publisher wishes to thank the following: Tim Burton, Scott Rudin, Adam Schroeder, Arthur Cohen, Nancy Goliger, Maren Moebius, Gretchen Lucas, BLT & Associates, Inc., Ricki Leigh Arnold, Rob Lebow, Michelle Johnson, Holly Rawlinson, Risa Kessler, Paul Ruditis, Melissa Obando, Phyllis Ungerleider

Sleepy Hollow production art supplied by Ravi Bansal, Mauro Borelli, Adam Brockbank, Martin Charles, Cosmas Demetriou, John Dexter, Rick Heinrichs, Michael Jackson, Simon Murton, Nick Navarro, Jonathon Rosen, Gerald Sullivan, Les Tomkins, Susan Wexler

Sleepy Hollow photography by Clive Coote, Jonathan Fisher, Peter Mountain, Alastair Thain, Pete Tangen, Industrial Light & Magic

INTRODUCTION

—

BY TIM BURTON

SLEEPY HOLLOW is one of those movies that has been kicking around in me for some time. Like a lot of people, I had known the story of the Headless Horseman mainly from the Disney cartoon. In Washington Irving's original short story, "The Legend of Sleepy Hollow," such an air pervades the town itself: Irving describes the sights and sounds of the Horseman that instill fear as "mere terrors of the night, phantoms of the mind that walk in the darkness." When I reread the story, so many elements came together: the Gothic setting, the air of mystery, and the sense that the town itself has a kind of sleepiness to it. Sleepy Hollow is a typical American farming community, but there's something a little off. It's almost as if the residents are caught in a dream, wrapped up completely in the folklore. No matter how you interpret the story, it's one of the few true American horror tales. I wanted to make a film that was respectful to the source material but also tapped into some of the visual influences of the classic Hammer horror films of the 1950s and 1960s. The outcome is a film that combines the distinct American aspects of a classic tale, but one presented with elements of the British horror-film tradition.

What I like about Andrew Kevin Walker's screenplay is that it honors the original story, but takes it into new territory. I also enjoy how the script reinvents the American icon of Ichabod Crane in an entirely new light. In our version, he's a New York City police constable rather than a schoolmaster, as in the original story. That provided us with whole new avenues to explore while retaining his somewhat "bookish" nature. As a character, and as a police officer, Ichabod is both behind the times and ahead of the times, and it's those contradictory aspects of his character that are fun and interesting. The story pits one iconic image—Ichabod—against another, that of the Headless Horseman. I don't quite know what the power is, but there is some reason why people always remember the Headless Horseman; he's a great figure of American literature and mythology. One of the original images in my mind was a character who lives in his head versus a character with no head. I always thought that was symbolically wonderful—the dichotomy of rational thought and science, at least as Ichabod sees it, versus the other reality of the Horseman, the ghoul, the unexplainable villain. Is he human or ghost; is he real or imagined?

It's always a great challenge to walk that line between the reality and the fantasy. My special thanks to the wonderful team of production designer Rick Heinrichs, costume designer Colleen Atwood, cinematographer Emmanuel Lubezki, and composer Danny Elfman. They and countless others have helped breathe new life into the Headless Horseman and awaken the town of Sleepy Hollow.

1 EXT. CITY STREETS—NIGHT

Empty cobblestone streets are bordered by stately buildings. A rapidly **CLANGING BELL** breaks the silence from afar.

INSERT TITLE: New York City
                                                          1799

TWO CONSTABLES clamor around a corner, lanterns held high, listening. They disappear down an alleyway.

2 EXT. CITY WATERFRONT—NIGHT

ELSEWHERE, piers border the Hudson. The **BELL** is **LOUDER** here. The two constables arrive, searching, pistols drawn.

                              CONSTABLE ONE
            Where are you?!

                              MAN'S VOICE (O.S.)
            Here . . . ! Over here!

The constables hurry to the river's edge . . .

Down an embankment, the **MAN**, another constable, has his back to us. He's waist deep in dark water, throwing aside his **ALARM BELL**, struggling to pull something from the murk . . .

                                    MAN
            I need your help with this.

Constable Two and Constable One move forward, wary.

                              CONSTABLE ONE
            Constable Crane? Ichabod Crane . . . is that you?

The **MAN** turns. Meet **ICHABOD CRANE**, handsome, eyes piercing but nervous and unsettled.

> ICHABOD
>
> None other, and not only me . . .
> (returns to lifting)
> I have found something . . .

Ichabod drags a bloated **MALE CORPSE** out from the water. He backs away, shaken, looks to the constables . . .

> ICHABOD (CONT'D)
>
> . . . which was lately a man.

3 INT. CITY WATCHHOUSE, JAIL—NIGHT

In a dank, cavernous room, the distinguished **HIGH CONSTABLE** lifts a blanket off the corpse in a wheelbarrow manned by Constable Two. Constable One and Ichabod are near, watching.

> HIGH CONSTABLE
>
> Burn it.

> CONSTABLE ONE
>
> Yes, sir.

Constable Two wheels the corpse down a **RAMP** to another room.

> ICHABOD
>
> Just a moment, if I may . . . we do not yet know the cause of death.

> HIGH CONSTABLE
>
> When you find 'em in the river, cause of death is drowning.

ICHABOD

Possibly so if there is water in the lungs, but . . . by pathology
we might determine whether or not he was dead when he went
into the river.

HIGH CONSTABLE

Cut him up? Are we heathens? Let him rest in peace—in one piece
as according to God and the New York Department of Health.

Ichabod is about to protest, but stops himself, frustrated.

Two **THUGGISH CONSTABLES**—different ones—bring in a bleeding **SEMICONSCIOUS MAN**.

HIGH CONSTABLE (CONT'D)

What happened to him?

THUGGISH CONSTABLE

Nothing, sir. Arrested for burglary.

The constables throw him against the bars of the slammer while one of them opens the cage door.
With their leather truncheons, the cops beat their prisoner into the cage and lock him in.

HIGH CONSTABLE

Good work . . .

Ichabod hurries to follow his two constables and the corpse.

4 EXT. CITY WATCHHOUSE—DAY

The metropolis thrives; horsedrawn vehicles plodding, **MEN**, **WOMEN** and **CHILDREN**,
MERCHANTS and **TRADESMEN** everywhere.

MEN are held in chains and gibbets in front of the Watchhouse.

5 INT. CITY WATCHHOUSE, JAIL—DAY

We enter midway into an "Audition Scene." A row of **CITY OFFICIALS** are "auditioning"
APPLICANTS (mostly obvious Cranks and Eccentrics) with Devices for crime fighting and crime
solving. The Applicants are crowded together to one side, waiting their turn. Ichabod, holding
only papers and books, is among them.

"On Stage" at this moment is an **INVENTOR** demonstrating his invention, of which more in a
moment. Facing the "stage" is the **BURGOMASTER**, flanked by the **HIGH CONSTABLE** (who has
a list of names) and various **MAGISTRATES** and **ALDERMEN**.

The Inventor is demonstrating a combination wallet and mousetrap.

INVENTOR

. . . and in a few weeks, the plague of pickpockets will be a thing
of the past!

He shows how to set the trap-spring.

> **INVENTOR (CONT'D)**
> Give me a dozen constables in gentleman's dress . . .

He pockets the wallet-trap.

> **INVENTOR (CONT'D)**
> . . . mixing with the crowds where pickpockets are rife!

He produces a fake hand-on-a-stick and does the business.

> **INVENTOR (CONT'D)**
> A stealthy hand dips into the gentleman's pocket . . . and—!

There is the sound of the trap snapping shut and the Inventor withdraws the fake hand with its fingers chopped off. The Officials wince, impressed.

> **BURGOMASTER**
> Thank you. We will take your device under consideration, Mr.
> Vanderbilt . . . Next!

A **SPOTTY MAN** starts dragging a man-size cage contraption to center stage . . . while Ichabod tries to get the attention of the Officials.

> **ICHABOD**
> Gentlemen!—the Millennium is almost upon us—In a few months we
> will be living in the nineteenth century—!

> **HIGH CONSTABLE**
> Wait your turn, Constable Crane—

> **ICHABOD**
> These devices are unworthy of a modern civilization . . .

> **BURGOMASTER**
> Quiet!—Next, I say!

> **SPOTTY MAN**
> Thank you, sir!

He turns proudly to his man-size cage, whose front hinges down for ingress.

The floor of the cage is a steel plate. A "writing board" for signing confessions is attached to the inside of the cage.

> **SPOTTY MAN (CONT'D)**
> The Tomkins self-locking Confessional is cheap at the price and will
> last for years with just an occasional wipe with a damp cloth . . . When
> the villain steps on the floor plate . . .

Ichabod, dropping books and papers around his feet, is feverishly writing on a blank page (his "traveling inkpot" is hung around his neck).

> **ICHABOD**
> (pointing to the Spotty Man)
> Arrest that man!

HIGH CONSTABLE
(jaw dropped)
Arrest . . . ?

ICHABOD
I accuse him of murder!

SPOTTY MAN
What the devil are you talking about, you loon?!

Ichabod takes two steps toward him and gives him a violent shove in the chest. The Spotty Man staggers back into his cage, which self-locks, and at the same time a head clamp descends from the top, gripping the Spotty Man's head. His arms flail about as he yells. Ichabod slaps his page on the writing board, offers his pen.

ICHABOD
Sign here!

SPOTTY MAN
(groaning and pointing)
The release handle . . .

ICHABOD
Not till you confess . . . !

Uproar around him, Ichabod waits as the prisoner signs the paper, then pulls the "release handle."

ICHABOD (CONT'D)
(waving the confession)
I have here a confession to the murder of a man I fished out of the river last night!

HIGH CONSTABLE
(furious)
Stand down!

ICHABOD
I stand up, for sense and justice! Our jails overflow with men and women convicted on confessions worth no more than this one!

The High Constable bangs a gavel until he gets some silence for the Burgomaster. Meanwhile, the Spotty Man is rescued by his friends.

BURGOMASTER
Constable, this is a song we have heard from you more than once but never before with this discordant accompaniment. I have two courses open to me. First, I can let you cool your heels in the cells until you learn respect for the dignity of my office . . .

ICHABOD
I beg pardon. I only meant well. Why am I the only one who sees that to solve crimes, to detect the guilty, we must use our brains?—to recognize vital clues, using up-to-date scientific—

BURGOMASTER
(interrupting)
Which brings me to the second course. Constable Crane, there is a town upstate, two days' journey to the north in the Hudson Highlands. It is a place called Sleepy Hollow. Have you heard of it?

ICHABOD
I have not.

BURGOMASTER
An isolated farming community, mostly Dutch. Three persons have been murdered there, all within a fortnight . . . each found with their head lopped off.

ICHABOD
Lopped off?

BURGOMASTER
Clean as dandelion heads, apparently. Now, these ideas of yours, they have never been put to the test . . .

ICHABOD
I have never been allowed to put them to the test!

BURGOMASTER
Just so, granted. So you take your experimentations to Sleepy Hollow and deduce, er detect the murderer. Bring him here to face our good justice. Will you do this?

ICHABOD
(swallowing doubt)
I shall, gladly.

BURGOMASTER
And remember—it is you, Ichabod Crane, who is now put to the test.

The Burgomaster smiles encouragingly.

6 INT/EXT. ICHABOD'S HOME, 2ND FLOOR—DAY (TITLE SEQUENCE BEGINS)

Piles of **BOOKS** and **PAPERS**, **JARS** of **CHEMICALS**, **MAGNIFYING GLASSES**, **CHALKBOARDS** covered with scrawl and **ANATOMY CHARTS** above a small bed.

AT THE WINDOW, Ichabod holds a bird cage with a red **CARDINAL** inside. He opens the cage and the bird flies free . . .

ICHABOD
Such a day for such a sad farewell. But, this is good-bye, my sweet . . .

Ichabod watches it go, sad, then looks down. A **COACH** halts in the street below. The forlorn **DRIVER** looks up.

7 EXT. NEW YORK CITY STREETS—DAY

ICHABOD'S COACH leaves city limits, forgoing civilization . . . following a dirt road to forested wilderness.

8 EXT. NEW YORK FORESTS—NIGHT

Coach lanterns light the way as the coach lumbers along, caressed by tight foliage. A **WOLF** is **HEARD HOWLING.** Ichabod looks out, unnerved, shuts the window's curtain.

9 EXT. UPSTATE FORESTS—DAY

The coach moves through sun dappled forest . . .

10 ICHABOD'S CITY COACH—DAY

Ichabod checks the contents of a **LEATHER SATCHEL** in his lap. He pauses a moment, studying the palm of his hand.

Ichabod touches strange **SCARS** on both his palms: evenly dispersed, tiny dots of tissue. Many scars. After a moment, he returns to looking through his satchel.

11 EXT. SLEEPY HOLLOW, THE LONG STRAIGHT ROAD—LATE DAY

Ichabod stands between two massive **STONE PILLARS.** He's unsure, turning to watch his coach leave him behind.

Ichabod picks up his bags and heads between the pillars, starting up a **LONG STRAIGHT ROAD.** He does not notice, in tree limbs above: **THREE DEAD RAVENS,** hung by twine.

12 EXT. SLEEPY HOLLOW, TOWN SQUARE—DUSK

Ichabod walks on, passing a **CHURCH** and **GRAVEYARD.** The road ahead is bordered by rows of businesses and two-story homes.

Ichabod enters the **TOWN SQUARE** proper. An **ELDERLY WOMAN** stands in a doorway, watching Ichabod. Ichabod tips his hat. The woman backs away, shuts her door.

Ichabod continues. He looks up . . . a **MAN** closes the shutters of a second-story window.

As Ichabod continues he sees that there are two or three Riflemen placed at vantage points on the roofs and also, when he looks back, a Rifleman up on the Church Tower. The whole village is like a Western town waiting for an attack.

13 EXT. WOODEN BUNKER—DUSK

A strange **WOODEN BUNKER,** like a small fortress with a **HUGE BELL** mounted on top, sits in a field. **SEVERAL DIRT FARMERS** are gathered, all with rifles.

Ichabod stops as he walks, looking at this . . .

A boy, **YOUNG MASBATH,** aged 10, comes to the Designated Rifleman, **JONATHAN MASBATH,** with food and drink, i.e., a picnic tied up in a cloth and a stone bottle of beer. Masbath Senior takes the picnic and gives Young Masbath an affectionate pat. He smiles confidently.

> **MASBATH SENIOR**
> Don't worry, son.

One farmer comes to lead Young Masbath away as Jonathan heads into the **BUNKER**, taking several rifles.

In front of the **BUNKER**, across a field, other dirt farmers light **TORCH POSTS** in a line along the forest edge.

Ichabod ponders this as he trudges along . . .

14 EXT. VAN TASSEL HOUSE—DUSK

Ahead on a hill: the grand Van Tassel **MANOR HOUSE**, windows aglow.

TITLE SEQUENCE ENDS

15 EXT. VAN TASSEL HOUSE, FRONT DOOR—NIGHT

Ichabod puts down his bags (a suitcase and a leather box-bag) but keeps his satchel.

JACK-O'-LANTERNS glow on the porch.

A **KISSING COUPLE** are lustfully busy in a dark corner of the porch. The woman is a pretty servant, **SARAH**. The man we will know as **DOCTOR LANCASTER**.

Ichabod almost blunders into them, causing a little panic and embarrassment, in which Ichabod shares, and as he mumbles apologies and opens the door, a shaft of light identifies the illicit couple for our further reference.

The open door reveals the **MAIN HALL** and **FOYER** . . .

There's a harvest party in progress. **PEOPLE** are gathered. **QUIET MUSIC** is **HEARD** from elsewhere.

16 INT. VAN TASSEL HOUSE, SITTING ROOM—NIGHT

Ichabod opens a door. **MEN** and **WOMEN** eat and drink, talking quietly in groups. Ichabod looks around, daunted, tentatively makes his way . . .

Ichabod bumps into a few people, excusing himself. He mops his sweaty brow, finds

ICHABOD
Pardon my intrusion, I seek Baltus Van Tassel but—

GIRL
In the parlor, sir, further on.

Ichabod thanks her, continues . . .

Ahead, **CHILDREN**, **YOUNG MEN** and **LADIES** in a circle taunt a **BLINDFOLDED YOUNG WOMAN** spun around by the handsome, barrel-chested man, **BROM VAN BRUNT**. Brom releases the woman. Everyone quiets, avoiding her searching hands.

The Blindfolded Woman circles slowly, chanting a **REFRAIN** that makes the **CHILDREN** and even some of the younger **WOMEN** shiver with pleasurable fright. They giggle nervously and hush each other up.

BLINDFOLDED WOMAN
"The Pickety Witch, the Pickety Witch, who's got a kiss for the PICKETY WITCH?"

She makes a lunge, grabbing empty air, just missing **BROM**; everyone moans humorously. Doctor Lancaster slips back into the party, and Sarah likewise.

Ichabod is trying to pass through to reach the farther door . . . and on the **NEXT REFRAIN** finds himself caught by the Blindfolded Woman.

Everyone stays quiet, that's the game, but of course everyone is also puzzled, not knowing Ichabod. The Woman touches Ichabod's face, which embarrasses Ichabod and displeases Brom.

CHILD

A kiss, a kiss!

WOMAN

She has to guess first.

The WOMAN is wifely, and as she puts her arm through Doctor Lancaster's arm, we realize she is his wife.

BLINDFOLDED WOMAN

Is it Theodore?

There's a general laugh at that.

ICHABOD

Pardon, ma'am, I am only a stranger.

BLINDFOLDED WOMAN

Then have a kiss on account.

She kisses him laughingly and takes the blindfold off to reveal a stunning beauty: KATRINA VAN TASSEL. She smiles. Ichabod tries to compose himself, stricken by the sight of her.

ICHABOD

I . . . um, I am looking for Baltus Van Tassel.

KATRINA

I am his daughter, Katrina Van Tassel.

BROM

And who are you, friend? We have not heard your name yet.

ICHABOD

I have not said it. Excuse me . . .

Brom grabs Ichabod's collar. Ichabod's baffled.

BROM

You need some manners.

KATRINA

Brom!

MAN'S VOICE (O.S.)

(admonishing)
Come, come—we want no raised voices . . .

We now SEE that the voice belongs to BALTUS VAN TASSEL, a working-class self-made Mr. Big with a sympathetic smile.

BALTUS (CONT'D)

It is only to raise the spirits during this dark time that I and my good
wife are giving this little party . . .

LADY VAN TASSEL stands behind him, a mix of homespun wife and well-kept lady. Brom releases Ichabod. Children hide behind Katrina. Ichabod's relieved to have a proper focal point. Others from the party gather.

> BALTUS (CONT'D)
> Young sir, you are welcome even if you are selling something!

This pleasantry relaxes the atmosphere around Ichabod.

> ICHABOD
> Thank you, sir. I am Constable Ichabod Crane, sent to you from New
> York with authority to investigate murder in Sleepy Hollow.

This has quite an effect. A man we will know as **MAGISTRATE PHILIPSE** looks up sharply. A man we will know as **REVEREND STEENWYCK** grunts skeptically. A man we have already seen, **DOCTOR LANCASTER**, exchanges a surprised look with another man, **NOTARY HARDENBROOK**.

> STEENWYCK
> (rudely)
> Well, what use is a Constable?!

Lady Van Tassel gives the Clergyman a reproachful look.

> LADY VAN TASSEL
> Then, Sleepy Hollow is grateful to you, Constable Crane—I hope you
> will honor this house by remaining with us until . . .

> BROM
> Until you've made the arrest!

To Ichabod's surprise this gets a nervous laugh. Baltus frowns at Brom. Katrina looks at Ichabod with renewed interest.

> BALTUS
> (to his wife)
> Well spoke!
> (to Ichabod)
> Come, sir. We'll get you settled.
> (to the Musicians)
> Play on!

Baltus catches the eye of Philipse, then of Lancaster, nodding as if to say "See you in a minute."

As he leads Ichabod out, he murmurs to Steenwyck, who nods and passes the murmur to Hardenbrook.

The Fiddlers strike up the music. Katrina watches Ichabod's exit. Brom watches Katrina's interest with displeasure.

17 INT. VAN TASSEL HOUSE, ICHABOD'S ROOM—NIGHT

We **HEAR** the music from downstairs. Ichabod is unpacking—arranging his scientific books. His "medical case," revealing a few mysterious Instruments of Detection, is open on the bed. Sarah is just delivering a pitcher of water to the washstand.

> ICHABOD
> Thank you. Please tell Mr. Van Tassel I will be down in a moment.

> SARAH
> I will, sir.
> (then—as she leaves)
> Thank God you are here!

Ichabod is a bit surprised by her emotion. Then he pours the water and douses his face.

20

18 INT. VAN TASSEL HOUSE, PARLOR—NIGHT

FIVE MEN wait grimly for Ichabod, silent in the presence of Sarah, who is placing a pipe cradle by Baltus. Lady Van Tassel is pouring the men a drink. The music from the party is faintly audible. Lancaster is 50, dour, always sweaty. Philipse is youngest, a drinker, eyes bloodshot, augmenting his glass with a shot from his private flask. Reverend Steenwyck has a disdainful, sour expression. Hardenbrook is oldest, ancient, nervous, one eye pale and blind.

> **HARDENBROOK**
> All the way from New York!

> **DOCTOR LANCASTER**
> A waste of time!

> **STEENWYCK**
> (to Baltus)
> What can he do?

> **BALTUS**
> (calmingly)
> Gentlemen, gentlemen . . .

Sarah, leaving, passes Doctor Lancaster, who secretly trails his hand against Sarah's buttock . . . not quite secretly enough for the vigilance of Lady Van Tassel, who, by the merest flick of an eye, shows us that she has noticed.

Sarah leaves just as Ichabod appears in the doorway, Sarah closing the door behind him.

> **BALTUS (CONT'D)**
> (to Ichabod)
> Excellent! Come in!
> (to his wife)
> Leave us, my dear.

> **ICHABOD**
> So. Three persons murdered. First, Peter Van Garrett and his son Dirk Van Garrett, both of them strong capable men, found together, decapitated. A week later, the Widow Winship, also decapitated. I will need to ask you many questions, but first let me ask—is anyone suspected?

21

The murderer is
and rides an

BALTUS

I don't understand you.

ICHABOD

I say, is there any one person suspect in these acts?

The men stir in their seats—their looks say "I told you so!"—"Useless!"—etc.

BALTUS

Constable . . . how much have your superiors explained to you?

ICHABOD

Only that the three were slain in open ground and their heads found severed from their bodies . . .

STEENWYCK

The heads were not found severed. The heads were not found at all.

ICHABOD

The heads are *gone*?

Hardenbrook leans forward, his voice cragged.

HARDENBROOK

Taken. Taken by the Headless Horseman. Taken back to hell.

ICHABOD

Pardon me, I . . . ?

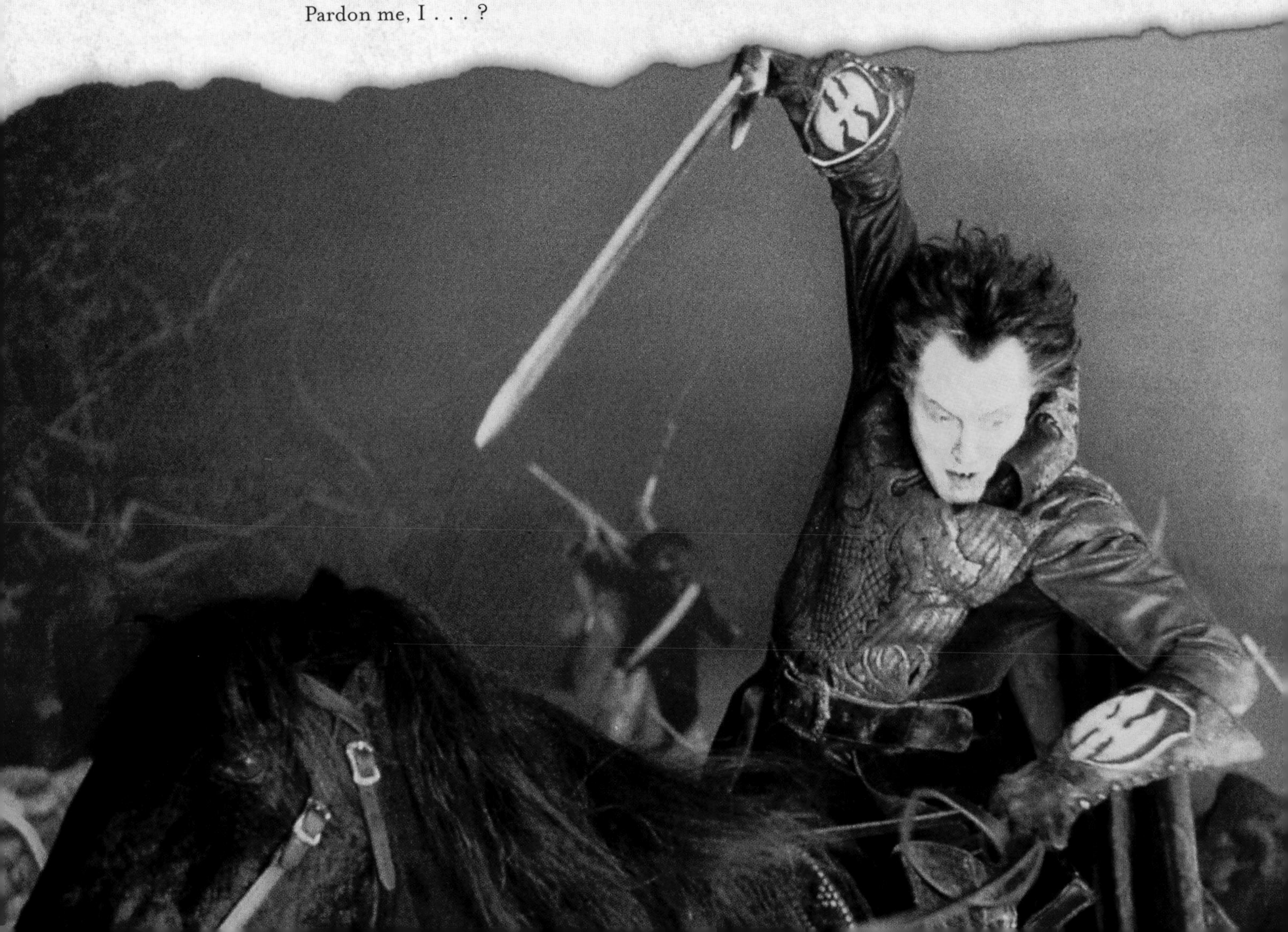

BALTUS

Perhaps you had better sit down.

Baltus gestures for Ichabod to sit. Baltus lights his pipe and pours a glass for Ichabod. The men help themselves to food and drink.

BALTUS (CONT'D)

The Horseman was a Hessian mercenary, sent to our shores by German princes to keep Americans under the yoke of England. But unlike his compatriots who came for money, the Horseman came . . . for love of carnage . . . and he was not like the others . . .

19 FLASHBACK—AMERICAN BATTLEFIELD (WINTER)—DAY

The **HESSIAN HORSEMAN** rides his black steed into a gory, close-quarters clash, his cloaked uniform adorned with edged weapons. He cuts down Americans left and right.

BALTUS (V.O.)

He rode a giant black steed named Daredevil. He was infamous for taking his horse hard into battle . . . chopping off heads at full gallop.

The Horseman dismounts, hoists a battle axe. With sword and axe, he annihilates. Blood gushes. Bones crack.

BALTUS (CONT'D; V.O.)
To look upon him made your blood run cold, for he had filed down his
teeth to sharp points . . . to add to the ferocity of his appearance . . .

The Horseman lets out a war cry. Jagged teeth. Grotesque.

20 FLASHBACK—FOREST BATTLEFIELD (WINTER)—DAY

Winter. **CANNONS** can be **HEARD BOOMING** from afar. Daredevil, galloping, is hit and falls.
The Horseman is not hurt.

BALTUS (V.O.)
This butcher would not finally meet his end till the winter
of seventy-nine . . .

The Horseman rises, eyes filled with rage, looks to see . . .

SIX ragtag **REVOLUTIONARY SOLDIERS** give chase, firing rifles. The Horseman flees, bullets
throwing snow behind.

BALTUS (CONT'D)
. . . not far from here in our Western Woods . . .

21 FLASHBACK—DEEPER IN THE FOREST BATTLEFIELD (WINTER)—DAY

The Horseman glances back, bounding through, drawing his sword, when suddenly he halts . . .

He's happened upon **TWO YOUNG GIRLS** gathering firewood. The girls stand frozen at the sight
of him for a long, silent moment, till one girl drops the firewood and runs.

26

The second girl remains, holding the Horseman's gaze.

The Horseman and the girl hold each other's gaze for a long beat.

The Horseman puts his finger to his lips, warning her to stay quiet.

The girl takes one of her pieces of dry wood and deliberately breaks it, making a noise like a pistol shot.

There is a responding shout from a soldier back in the trees. The Horseman turns to the sound.

Soldiers move forward from the forest behind, spreading out.

The second girl flees. The Horseman hefts his sword, turning as soldiers surround. One soldier aims his rifle . . .

The Horseman reaches over his shoulder, grasps a sheathed knife and **THROWS—**

THOCK! The rifleman jerks back, knife in his eye socket.

A second soldier aims and **FIRES** . . . Blood explodes from the Horseman's arm. His sword drops.

The Horseman readies an **AXE** in his good hand. The Revolutionaries move in with swords. They battle, **STEEL AGAINST STEEL**. The Horseman fends off blows . . .

Soldier Three stabs his blade deep into the Horseman's side. The Horseman roars, bringing his axe **DOWN** . . .

BREAKS the sword at the hilt. An **UPWARD** stroke sends Soldier Three backward in a fountain of blood.

The Horseman staggers, trying to pull the blade from his ribs. The remaining soldiers close in . . .

22 INT. VAN TASSEL HOUSE, PARLOR—NIGHT

Ichabod is spooked. Pipe smoke wafts from Baltus's mouth.

> **BALTUS**
> They cut off his head with his own sword. To this day, the Western
> Woods is a haunted place where brave men will not venture.

23 FLASHBACK—EXT. WESTERN WOODS TREE OF THE DEAD AREA (WINTER)—DAY

The Horseman's headless corpse lies in a shallow grave.

> **BALTUS (V.O.)**
> . . . for what was planted in the ground that day was a seed of evil.

The **HORSEMAN'S HEAD** is dropped into the grave.

24 FLASHBACK—EXT. WESTERN WOODS TREE OF THE DEAD AREA
   (WINTER)—LATER DAY

One of the four surviving soldiers stabs the **HORSEMAN'S SWORD** deep in the ground as a marker.

The grave is done. The soldiers walk away from the grave. They have buried the Horseman in a treeless clearing.

Daredevil appears, limping, from the trees, and puts his nose down to the turned earth.

The Second Girl is watching from hiding.

She sees: Daredevil collapses on the grave, blood frothing from his mouth. Dying.

25 INT. VAN TASSEL HOUSE, PARLOR—NIGHT

> BALTUS
>
> And so it has been for twenty years. But now the Hessian wakes—he is on the rampage, cutting off heads where he finds them.

Ichabod sits back, shakes off the reverie of the tale. He takes a gulp from his glass.

> ICHABOD
>
> Are you . . . saying . . . ? Is that what you believe?

> HARDENBROOK
>
> Seeing is believing!

Baltus puts a calming hand on senile Hardenbrook's shoulder.

> DOCTOR LANCASTER
>
> No one knows why the Hessian has chosen this time to return from the grave.

> STEENWYCK
>
> Satan has called forth one of his own.

Steenwyck stands and from a side table picks up the hefty Baltus family Bible.

> STEENWYCK (CONT'D)
>
> They tell me you have brought books and trappings of scientific investigation—this is the only book I recommend you study.

He drops the Bible on the table in front of Ichabod, making him jump. Ichabod gingerly lifts the front cover—revealing a page of ink writing, which he will remember later—then he snaps out of all this "nonsense."

> ICHABOD
>
> Reverend Steenwyck . . . gentlemen . . . murder needs no ghost come from the grave. Which of you have laid eyes on this Headless Horseman?

Pause.

> HARDENBROOK
>
> Others have. Many others.

Ichabod allows himself a skeptical smile.

> BALTUS
>
> You will see him too if he comes again. The men of the village are posted to watch for him.

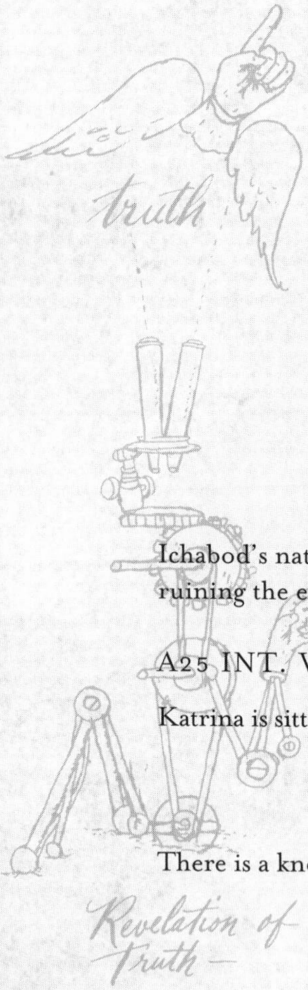

ICHABOD

We have murders in New York without benefit of ghouls and goblins.

BALTUS

You are a long way from New York, sir.

ICHABOD

A century at least. The assassin is a man of flesh and blood, and I will discover him.

STEENWYCK

How do you propose to do so?

ICHABOD

By discovering his reason. It is what we call "the motive." This mystery will not resist investigation by a Rational Man.

Ichabod's natural nervous clumsiness, however, causes him to sweep his empty glass off the table, rather ruining the effect of the Rational Man in command of the situation.

A25 INT. VAN TASSEL HOUSE, KATRINA'S ROOM—NIGHT

Katrina is sitting in front of her mirror. Lady Van Tassel is brushing out Katrina's hair, counting the strokes.

KATRINA

Well, I'm disappointed . . . our first visitor from New York . . .

There is a knock.

KATRINA (CONT'D)

He doesn't know where to put himself and his feet are all over the place.

Lady Van Tassel gives Katrina the hairbrush and goes to the door.

LADY VAN TASSEL

Yes, not like your Brom. Go on brushing, I got to forty-four . . .

She opens the door to Sarah.

SARAH

That constable, he wants the Bible, Mum . . .

LADY VAN TASSEL

Bible . . . ?

KATRINA

I'll bring it to him.

Sarah dips a curtsy and goes. Lady Van Tassel gives Katrina a friendly raised eyebrow.

KATRINA (CONT'D)
(meeting her eye, explains)
We'll see if his city talk fits him better than his clothes.

26 INT. VAN TASSEL HOUSE, ICHABOD'S ROOM—NIGHT

Ichabod sits surrounded by his books, including his Ledger. Clearly there has been no breakthrough. Ichabod broods. There is a knock at the door, which he seems to have been expecting, for he does not turn around.

ICHABOD

Yes—yes—come in.

Katrina enters carrying the Bible.

ICHABOD (CONT'D)
(not turning)
Thank you, just leave it on the reading stand.

Katrina puts down the Bible as directed.

ICHABOD (CONT'D)
That will be all—no, tell me, about that big brute who seems to be
Miss Katrina's—

He has turned in his chair, too late, and sees Katrina—Ichabod has a minor convulsion, standing up, knocking papers to the floor, etc.

ICHABOD (CONT'D)

Forgive me, I . . . I asked Sarah to bring me . . .

KATRINA

(amused, relaxed)

So your clever books have failed you and you turn to the Bible after all!

ICHABOD

(sharply, despite himself)

I see I am talked about downstairs.

KATRINA

In passing only—we have many things to talk about even in this backward place.

ICHABOD

I am sorry . . . Please excuse my manner—I am not used to . . .

KATRINA

Female company?

ICHABOD

Society.

KATRINA

How can you avoid society in New York? How I should love the opera—
and theaters—to go dancing . . . Is it wonderful?

ICHABOD

I have never been.

KATRINA

But there is an art museum?—a concert hall?

ICHABOD

I don't know.

KATRINA
(disappointed)
Then you have nothing to teach me.

ICHABOD
Perhaps I have. Do you believe the Van Garretts and the Widow Winship
were murdered by a headless horseman?

KATRINA
Not everyone here believes it is the Horseman.

ICHABOD
(relieved)
Good.

KATRINA
Some say it is the witch of the Western Woods who has made a pact with
Lucifer.

ICHABOD
(exasperated)
There are no witches, or galloping ghosts either! Is everyone in this village
in thrall to superstition?

KATRINA
Why are you so frightened of magic? Not all magic is black. There are
ancient truths in these woods which have been forgotten in your city parks.

ICHABOD
If they are truths they are not magic—and if magic, not truth.

KATRINA
You are foolish. When there is fever in the house, it is well known that willow-
herb roots and a crow's foot must be boiled in the milk of a pure white goat
with special charms uttered over the fire . . . and the fever abates.

ICHABOD
Next time try the herb without the rest—and now I must ask you—excuse me—

KATRINA
Gladly. I should not have interrupted our town's savior. Good night. And as to
your first question, that big brute you were asking about has proposed to me.

ICHABOD
I . . . I . . . I'm happy that . . .

KATRINA
Proposed to me several times.

This ambiguous statement, accompanied by a faint smile, confuses Ichabod into silence as she closes the door
behind her. He turns with relief to the next business—the Bible. He opens the front cover. On the endpaper
is a Family Tree going back a hundred years, in variously faded inks and handwritings.

Ichabod studies it and we see what he learns: that Katrina was born in 1777 . . . to Baltus's first wife, who
died in 1797 . . . that Lady Van Tassel is Baltus's second wife (her maiden name is unimportant, because
false) . . . Then he suddenly notices something even more interesting: The family tree has a "Van Garrett"
in it—the husband of Baltus's father's sister.

ICHABOD
(mutters)
Van Garrett . . . !

Ichabod looks thoughtful. He starts copying out details into his Ledger.

A very faint rumbling disturbs him for a moment. He looks up. Silence now. He continues working.

27 EXT. SLEEPY HOLLOW—NIGHT

The empty street.

Then the low sinister sound of rumbling is heard again.

28 EXT. WOODEN BUNKER FIELD—INTERCUT—NIGHT

The distant **SOUND** of the **GROUND RUMBLING** is **HEARD. AT THE WOODEN BUNKER**, Jonathan looks out, fearful . . .

The torches burn bright along the forest line. **SEVERAL DEER** stampede out . . . sprinting across the field.

Jonathan watches the forest. A horrible, **SILENT** stillness has fallen. Then, Jonathan's eyes widen . . .

A thick **FOG** creeps from the woods.

As fog overtakes each torch, mist snakes up, snuffing each flame . . . one by one by one, all along the forest edge . . .

Jonathan sticks his rifle out from the bunker, sights the gun along the treeline.

JONATHAN
Come out, devil . . . come . . .

29 EXT. SLEEPY HOLLOW FORESTS, OVERVIEW—NIGHT

Silhouetted treetops. The **SOUNDS** of **JONATHAN'S RIFLE FIRING** are **HEARD**, echoing—**SEVERAL GUNSHOTS**, then . . . **SILENCE** . . .

30 EXT. SLEEPY HOLLOW FOREST—NIGHT

Jonathan flees through the forest, glances back, terrified. **THUNDEROUS HOOFBEATS** are **HEARD** from behind.

DEEP IN THE FOREST, we **GLIMPSE** the source of the **HOOFBEATS**: a **HUGE FORM** on a **HUGE BLACK HORSE**, already gone.

Jonathan pushes through thorny bushes. Jagged branches bloody his hands and cheeks . . .

He bursts from the brier patch and **TUMBLES** to a **TRAIL.**

IN THE FOREST BEHIND: The hooves of the black horse rip underbrush. **HOOFBEATS DEAFENING.** A spur digs into the snorting steed's already bleeding flank.

The pursuer's gloved hand draws a **SWORD,** blade **RINGING.**

ON THE TRAIL, Jonathan runs onward. The shrill **WHISTLE** of a **SWORD SWING** is **HEARD** as the pursuer **BLURS PAST** . . .

Jonathan is still running when his head lolls back, at an impossible angle . . . his head tumbles off his shoulders . . .

Jonathan's headless body hits the dirt.

A30 EXT. SLEEPY HOLLOW—DAY (EARLY MORNING)

People going about their business calmly. A **WOMAN** shakes out a blanket from an upper window. The murder has obviously not been discovered yet.

No one notices that the **WOODEN BUNKER** is deserted . . . and now has a gap of shattered timber.

31 EXT/INT. LIVERY STABLE—DAY (EARLY MORNING)

The stables belong to **KILLIAN,** a dashingly rustic man, father of a young family. Ichabod likes him . . . though he does not think much of the Horse Killian is offering him, an old nag. Ichabod has a big satchel.

> KILLIAN
>
> His name's Gunpowder.

> ICHABOD
>
> A brave name, but . . . have you got something a little
> younger? . . . Taller?

> KILLIAN
> (apparently getting it)
> Faster.

> ICHABOD
>
> Yes.

> KILLIAN
>
> A horse to cut a dash.

> ICHABOD
>
> Yes.

KILLIAN

No, I haven't.

ICHABOD

Oh.

KILLIAN

Not at the price.

ICHABOD

Well . . . I'm sure he'll do very well. Thank you, Mr. Killian.

KILLIAN

Good luck, sir. If you need help, call my name.

ICHABOD

Much appreciated.

Killian's son Thomas, a small boy, is feeding one of the horses.

ANGLE ON MRS. KILLIAN at the door of the Killian House. She is in the act of seeing a woman out of her door, a **PREGNANT WOMAN**, and handing her a bunch of herbs.

CLOSER

BETH

(to Pregnant Woman)
Mind you rub them well in the breech, Mrs. Sherry—don't worry,
it'll be easy as shelling peas.

As the Pregnant Woman leaves, Beth bawls over her shoulder, turning to go into the house.

BETH (CONT'D)

Thomas!—It's you I want!

Beth goes into the house, passing a modest notice on the door: *"Knock before entering—Elizabeth Killian, MIDWIFE"*

KILLIAN

(to Thomas)
Go off home for your breakfast, Tom—kiss your mother once for you
and twice for me.

As the boy goes, Ichabod has a thought.

ICHABOD

Mr. Killian, I was thinking . . . about the old widow . . .

KILLIAN

Old Widow?

ICHABOD

Widow Winship.

KILLIAN

Who told you she was old? She was comely. Widowed young and dead
before the bloom was off her.

Ichabod is surprised. Before he can react further, a distant gunshot is heard—
a signal followed by the distant sight of a man on horseback, hurrying and
shouting, waving his rifle. It's clear that Masbath's murder has been discovered.
Killian and Ichabod watch the Rider coming, telling the news as he comes.

> RIDER
> (shouting)
> Murder, murder! The Horseman has
> killed again!

32 EXT. SLEEPY HOLLOW FARMLAND—DAY

Riders are galloping across the fields toward the murder site . . .

Baltus, a Dullardly Man called VAN RIPPER, who was the original Rider who
found the body . . . followed by Brom, and a gig driven fast by Philipse,
and Doctor Lancaster and various villagers.

Way behind, trying to keep up on Gunpowder, comes Ichabod.

33 EXT. FOREST, MASBATH MURDER SITE—MORNING

Baltus takes charge of posting armed villagers to keep an eye out toward
the forest.

> BALTUS
> Mr. Miller—ride back for the coffin cart—
> the rest of you keep a sharp lookout.
> (to GLEN)
> No—not at me, Glen, I'm not going to cut
> my own head off!—Look to the woods!

Ichabod hasn't quite arrived. The others are watching as Doctor Lancaster
turns over the headless corpse of Masbath. He straightens the body reverently.
Everyone is shocked and spooked, looking fearfully around. Behind them—
a sound. Everyone reacts but it's Ichabod arriving.

> BROM
> (laughs)
> A fine looking animal, Crane.

Ichabod dismounts, ignoring Brom. The great Detective is trying to cover up
his jitters. New York was never like this.

> DOCTOR LANCASTER
> The fourth victim, Jonathan Masbath.

> ICHABOD
> And . . . the head . . . ?

> PHILIPSE
> Taken.

ICHABOD

Taken!

Doctor Lancaster seems unprofessionally jittery. He grasps Philipse by the arm. Philipse shakes him off and pulls out a flask. Ichabod notices this. Their behavior seems to him to be an odd moment. Then he turns his attention back to the matter at hand.

ICHABOD (CONT'D)

Interesting . . . very interesting.

BALTUS

What is?

ICHABOD

In headless corpse cases of this sort . . . the head is removed to prevent identification of the body.

BALTUS

(puzzled)
But we know this is Jonathan Masbath . . .

ICHABOD

Exactly! So, why was the head removed?

They all wait for enlightenment.

BALTUS

Why?

ICHABOD

I don't know.

They all watch Ichabod to see what he will do. Philipse takes nips from his flask. But Ichabod isn't sure. He isn't too keen on looking at the corpse. Then he realizes:

ICHABOD (CONT'D)

You have moved the body?

DOCTOR LANCASTER

I did.

ICHABOD

(furious)
You must never move the body!

DOCTOR LANCASTER

Why not?

ICHABOD

Because!

Despite themselves, they are impressed. Ichabod takes heart.

Ichabod finds a huge, deep **HOOFPRINT**. He kneels, pulls his satchel off his shoulder, takes out a **BOWL**, **BOTTLE** of **WATER** and a **BAG** of **POWDER**.

The others watch, finding this bizarre, as Ichabod begins mixing the water and powder, making plaster.

BROM

What is that potion?

ICHABOD

You are the blacksmith, Brom. Ever shoe a horse with a hoof this large?

Ichabod fills the print with runny plaster.

BROM

(grudging the point)
It's big.

Ichabod shoulders his satchel, walks all around, studies the ground, kicks away leaves . . . and then lopes around puzzlingly. The watchers are astonished by his antics as he leaps from hoofprint to hoofprint.

DOCTOR LANCASTER

(to Philipse)
The man's a fool.

PHILIPSE

(drunk)
He's a fool and we're damn fools—but death will make us all equal.

Doctor Lancaster impatiently hushes him and turns away.

ICHABOD

The stride is gigantic . . .

Ichabod stops, turns, following back the way he came . . .

ICHABOD (CONT'D)

The attacker rode Masbath down . . . turned his horse . . .
came back . . .
(stops leaping)
Came back to claim the head.

He pauses to sum up.

ICHABOD (CONT'D)

To sum up. Head taken. Big horse.
(beat)
Did this man have any enemies?

PHILIPSE

Well, someone didn't like him.

But Ichabod has already latched on to something.

ICHABOD

Van Ripper, show me where the neck rested.

Van Ripper points. Ichabod opens his satchel, takes out a **BOTTLE OF GREEN POWDER**.

He uncorks the bottle, sprinkles a thin layer of powder on the dirt, waiting.

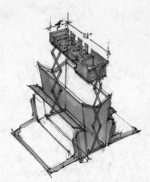

41

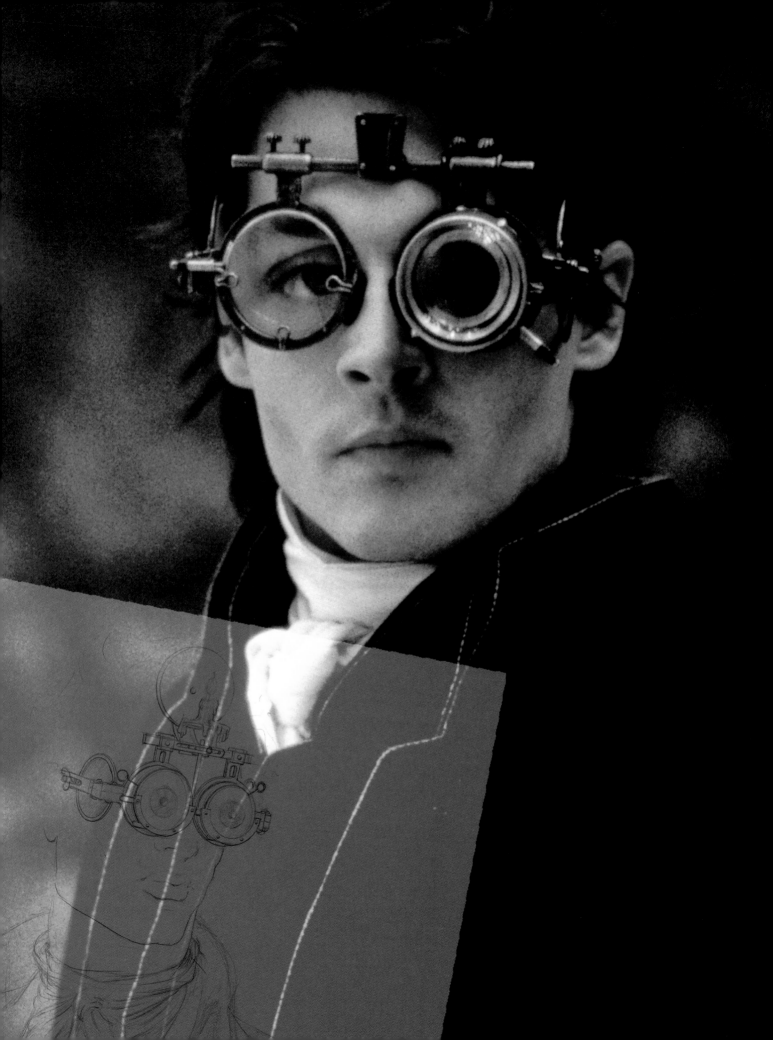

A reaction causes the powder to bubble a little.

> ICHABOD (CONT'D)
> A chemical reaction, it shows there was just a smear
> of blood, no more.

> VAN RIPPER
> I didn't see none.

Ichabod's puzzled.

Ichabod swallows, queasy, trying not to let it show.

Ichabod takes odd spectacles from his satchel, wire-framed with many lenses: **MAGNIFICATION SPECTACLES**. He fumbles putting them on, examines the gross neck wound.

Ichabod takes an **INSTRUMENT** from his satchel, a delicate **SCISSOR MECHANISM TOOL** that tapers off to tiny jaws. He uses it, hand shaking, to pick at the flesh.

POV through Ichabod's magnifying spectacles: a **CREEPY CRAWLY BUG** is feeding on the wound. Ichabod freaks, leaps up.

> ICHABOD
> (recovering, faking)
> Interesting . . .

> BALTUS
> What is it?—What is it?!

Squinting sidelong at the ground, Ichabod uses his foot to squash and grind the bug, which is too small to be visible.

He looks at Baltus, his eyes huge in his spectacles.

> ICHABOD
> The wound was cauterized in the very
> instant . . . as though the blade itself were red
> hot . . . and yet, no blistering, no scorched flesh.

They all look worried.

> PHILIPSE
> The Devil's fire!

Ichabod looks worried too.

Binocular glasses

34 EXT. CEMETERY—DAY

The town is gathered for Jonathan Masbath's funeral. Steenwyck stands at the open grave, reads from the **BIBLE**.

> **STEENWYCK**
> (reading)
> "Be sober, be vigilant . . ." as it sayeth in the book of Peter, chapter five, verse eight—"because your adversary the devil, as a roaring lion, walketh about, seeking whom he may devour . . ."

People **WHISPER** and steal glances at Ichabod. Ichabod stands with Baltus and Lady Van Tassel. Ichabod looks around, observing . . .

Young Masbath stands with his head bowed.

Brom stands beside Katrina, who wipes tears. Brom puts his arm around Katrina, comforting. Theodore and Glenn are nearby with rifles over their shoulders.

35 EXT. CEMETERY/CHURCH—(TIME CUT)—LATER DAY

The funeral is done. People head out from the cemetery.

Ichabod walks with the Van Tassels. Baltus holds Katrina's hand. Young Masbath runs to catch up with Ichabod.

> **YOUNG MASBATH**
> Mister Constable, sir . . .

Ichabod stops.

> **ICHABOD**
> You are Young Masbath . . .

> **YOUNG MASBATH**
> I was Young Masbath, but now the only one. Masbath at your service, in honor bound to avenge my father.

> **ICHABOD**
> Well, one-and-only Masbath, I thank you, but your mother will need you more than I.

> **YOUNG MASBATH**
> My mother is in heaven, sir, and has my father now to care for her. But you have no one to serve you, and I am your man, sir.

> **ICHABOD**
> And a brave man too, but I cannot be the one to look after you. I am sorry for your loss, young Mister Masbath.

Ichabod moves away, watched disconsolately by Masbath.

Ichabod finds his sleeve furtively plucked by Philipse.

> **PHILIPSE**
>
> Constable . . .

> **ICHABOD**
>
> Mr. Philipse . . . ?

Philipse looks around anxiously to see if they're observed.

> **PHILIPSE**
>
> Something you should know. Jonathan Masbath was not the fourth
> victim but the fifth!

> **ICHABOD**
>
> The fifth?

> **PHILIPSE**
>
> Aye. Five victims in four graves!

> **ICHABOD**
>
> But who . . . ?

Philipse sees that Steenwyck has noticed the encounter. He breaks off and scuttles away.

Ichabod turns his gaze toward . . .

The fresh grave of Jonathan Masbath, and three more graves almost as recent:
The Van Garretts are just receiving their brand new headstones, and Widow Winship's
grave is marked for the present by a simple wooden cross with her name on it.

Ichabod sees Killian and nods to him.

> **ICHABOD (CONT'D)**
>
> Mr. Killian . . . I will need the help you offered.

36 INT. STABLE—DAY

Ichabod lifts the lid of a large feed bin half full of horse feed. Young Masbath is curled up
inside like a mouse in a nest. Homeless.

> **ICHABOD**
>
> Find a place in the Van Tassel's servant quarters. Wake me
> before dawn. I hope you have a strong stomach.

Ichabod walks away, disgruntled.

> **YOUNG MASBATH**
>
> Thank you, sir.

37 EXT. CEMETERY—NIGHT/DAWN

The lid of a muddy coffin is wrenched open. The coffin contains a headless corpse. Just the one.

What's happening?

The coffin is on the ground next to the hole marked by the headstone of Peter Van Garrett.

Killian holds a lantern and a spade. Ichabod, holding a handkerchief to his face, looks into the open
coffin. He nods. Ichabod, in shirtsleeves and sweating, has a spade too. Young Masbath is watching
uneasily. This is why Young Masbath would need a "strong stomach." He gags, almost pukes.

45

At Ichabod's nod, Killian replaces the lid. Killian has Two Men with him. There are two more coffins and two more piles of dirt, one coffin for Dirk Van Garrett and one for Widow Winship.

Ichabod moves to the second coffin. It contains a headless corpse. Just the one. Ichabod nods, and the lid is replaced.

The third coffin—the Widow's—is being opened by one of the Men. Ichabod takes a lantern and looks expectantly as the lid comes off. The Widow's headless corpse is alone in the coffin.

Ichabod pauses. Nods. As the lid is about to be replaced. He stops it.

ICHABOD

Wait.

Ichabod takes out a small penknife and cuts through the shroud. He reveals the belly. He stares at it. Was she pregnant? It's impossible to tell. But there is the wound of a sword stab in the stomach.

Suddenly there is a screech, which seems to come from the corpse, giving heart attacks all around—but now we see a "ghost" holding a lantern. It's Reverend Steenwyck who has discovered them and is shrieking in outrage.

STEENWYCK

Sacrilege! Sacrilege!

Ichabod recovers.

ICHABOD

Science . . . science, Reverend Steenwyck! Someone in Sleepy Hollow
is using the Horseman story for his own murderous purpose, and I
intend to . . . dig it out!

Steenwyck froths, looks terrified and backs off.

38 INT. DOCTOR'S RESIDENCE, MEDICAL ROOM—DAY

Ichabod and Killian, helped by Young Masbath, carry the Widow's muddy coffin inside. Doctor Lancaster watches in horror, sweating profusely, freaked out.

DOCTOR LANCASTER

This is . . . most irregular, Constable.

> ICHABOD

I should hope so, Doctor. But in this case, necessary.

The coffin is put down.

> ICHABOD (CONT'D)
> (importantly)

I will need to operate.

> DOCTOR LANCASTER

Operate? She's dead!

> ICHABOD
> (thrown)

When we say "operate," we mean, of course . . . er, I'll need the
operating table. Lay her out, please.
> (to Young Masbath)
Go on, nothing to be afraid of.

While Killian and Young Masbath lay out the corpse, Ichabod gulps water and studies the pages
of his Ledger.

> ICHABOD (CONT'D)

There is a common thread between these victims.

> DOCTOR LANCASTER

And what's that?

> ICHABOD
> (closing the Ledger)

I don't know.

He goes to examine the corpse. Young Masbath retreats to a corner, ill at ease.

> ICHABOD (CONT'D)

Once more, the neck wound cauterized. The sword thrust to the
stomach, the same, perhaps by chemical means. But to what purpose?

Ichabod gingerly feels the corpse's stomach. The Doctor watches. We get the feeling he "knows something."

> DOCTOR LANCASTER

To what is your purpose, is the question.

Ichabod takes a rolled VELVET CLOTH from his satchel, unrolls it . . . it holds SURGICAL
INSTRUMENTS, some particularly strange: RIB-SPREADERS and CURVED CLAMPS.

> DOCTOR LANCASTER (CONT'D)

What manner of instruments are those?

> ICHABOD

Some of my own design.

Ichabod picks through his instruments, unsure. He looks to the corpse a long moment.
He looks at Young Masbath.

> ICHABOD (CONT'D)

Step outside. Thank you for your help, Mr. Killian. And, if you do
not mind, Doctor, my concentration suffers when I am observed.

48

Ichabod watches Killian, Young Masbath and Lancaster go. He quickly returns to his satchel, pulling out a **BOOK**: *HUMAN ANATOMY*. He searches the pages . . .

He flips through **DRAWINGS** of **ANATOMY**, then sets the book open nearby so he can refer to it. He picks up a **KNIFE**, stands at the corpse, taking a deep uncertain breath.

Ichabod cuts into the Widow's belly, but stops, looking horrified at what he's done. He leans close to study the book again, worried. He makes another incision . . . He looks down at it, queasy.

39 EXT. DOCTOR'S RESIDENCE—DAY

Young Masbath sits waiting.

Doctor Lancaster stands with Philipse (hung over), Steenwyck and Hardenbrook, speaking agitatedly. **OTHER PEOPLE** have gathered in the background.

The door to the doctor's residence opens and Ichabod steps out. He is bloodied, shaken, futilely wiping at the mess with a blood-covered cloth, looking up . . .

All attention goes to Ichabod. Everyone's horrified.

ICHABOD

I am . . . finished.

STEENWYCK

What in God's name have you done to her?

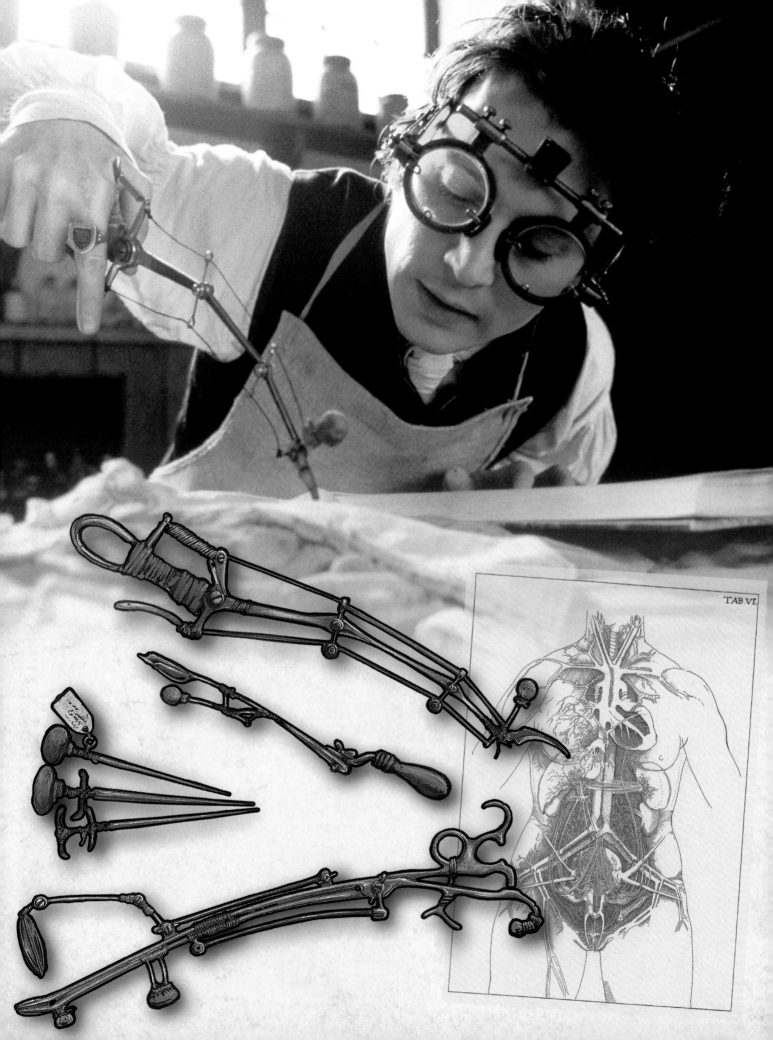

TAB.VI

(pointing)
Magistrate Philipse, you are the word of law here . . . put him
in irons!

Philipse and Ichabod exchange a look. Philipse nips from his flask.

PHILIPSE
And what did you find out, Constable?

ICHABOD
That there are not four victims but five. The Widow Winship was
with child!

The small crowd murmurs, shocked. Doctor Lancaster recovers, furious.

DOCTOR LANCASTER
What of it? She should have been left to make her peace with God
and not cut to bits by the Constabulary!

Ichabod is shaken for a moment, remembering the similar charge made against him in New York.

ICHABOD
The sword was thrust into the womb and no farther. A symbolic
murder. We are dealing with a madman.

40 EXT. LONG STRAIGHT ROAD, COVERED BRIDGE—LATER NIGHT

Pale moonlight. Ichabod rides Gunpowder across the **COVERED BRIDGE**. They are an ungainly pair.

Following the road, Ichabod is lost in thought. The **CLOPPING** of **HOOFBEATS** is **HEARD** on the
bridge behind.

Ichabod turns to look. **HOOFBEATS STOP**. No one can be seen in the dark mouth of the bridge.
CRICKETS CHIRP.

ICHABOD
Who's there?

Ichabod faces forward, continuing to the forest.

He hums a tune to himself, tone deaf. After a moment, a **HORSE** is **HEARD SNORTING**,
HOOFBEATS RESUME. Ichabod stops Gunpowder.

There is **SOMEONE** back there, on horseback, coming out from the darkness of the bridge, slowly . . .

ICHABOD (CONT'D)
Who are you?

The **FIGURE** comes into moonlight, on a **BLACK HORSE**, smoke seeming to rise from him; a dark
FIGURE, cloaked—headless.

Ichabod panics, kicking Gunpowder to flee. The figure takes off to follow.

Ichabod whips Gunpowder's reins, gasping, moving faster. The figure behind also picks up speed.

41 EXT. SLEEPY HOLLY FOREST—NIGHT

Gunpowder carries Ichabod into the forest. The headless figure is right behind, cloak flowing . . .

The **HEADLESS FIGURE** is **HEARD** letting out a hellish **CRY** of rage. Ichabod glances fearfully over his shoulder . . .

A **HORRIBLE FACE** with flaming eyes and mouth rushes forward . . .

It **SMASHES** into Ichabod—sends him sprawling to the ground in an explosion of red hot ash and cinders . . .

Ichabod rolls, shaken . . . looking behind. The trail is empty. **HOOFBEATS** are **HEARD**. **SEVERAL HORSES**.

Ichabod stands. He looks down at the remnants of a **BROKEN JACK-O'-LANTERN** and smoldering ball of paper on the trail.

The **FIGURE** rides to a halt, throws off a cloak and "headless" disguise; it's Brom. Glenn and Theodore ride up, laughing.

Brom also laughs, but when he looks back, the smile leaves his face. He takes grim satisfaction in what he's done.

Ichabod's face is haunted, running with the sweat of fear—he is still trembling from the experience.

> **FEMALE VOICE (V.O.)**
> Ichabod! Ichabod!

And suddenly we are pitched into Ichabod's **DREAM**.

43 ICHABOD'S DREAM—EXT. COTTAGE—DAY

> **FEMALE VOICE (V.O.)**
> Ichabod! Ichabod . . . !

A woman is in the doorway, holding out her arms. She seems to be Katrina as Ichabod first saw her, blindfolded.

A YOUNG BOY, aged about seven, runs toward her, with a little bunch of wildflowers.

44 ICHABOD'S DREAM—YOUNG ICHABOD'S KITCHEN—NIGHT

The Blindfolded Woman is playing the Pickety Witch Game with Ichabod. He is laughing—scared as she grabs the air looking for him. He is holding the wildflowers he picked. She seizes him, kisses him and takes off the blindfold. It's not Katrina, but his Mother, a kind and lovely face. He gives his Mother the flowers. She puts one of the flowers in her hair, laughing. But the others—she throws on the fire!—and she crouches at the hearthstone, beckoning him, still "nice." He comes to her, not scared.

As the flowers burn, they give off smoky fumes, which the Mother inhales like perfume, closing her eyes in a trance. He watches fascinated as she picks up a twig and starts drawing pictures—strange designs—in the layer of ash on the hearthstone.

Suddenly Ichabod turns his head to the door, which is opening—spooky because no one is entering. Then he sees at floor level the family **CAT** has come through the door. A black cat with a white paw.

Ichabod's Mother is "awakened" by this, just in time as Father, a grim Parson all in black, enters.

Ichabod looks up frightened at the face of his Father.

45 ICHABOD'S DREAM—YOUNG ICHABOD'S BEDROOM—NIGHT

The Cat is on Ichabod's bed . . . watching Mother who is entertaining Ichabod with the Bird-in-Cage Spinning Disc Toy, which we will get to know.

Ichabod is tucked up in bed, astonished and happy. The Bird and Cage blur together.

Lightning flashes outside a window, thunder booms, the storm bursts open the window.

The Cat leaps off the bed, caught in lightning flash, the Toy drops, tangled on the bed. Ichabod covers his face, scared; his Mother hugs him.

46 INT. VAN TASSEL HOUSE, ICHABOD'S ROOM—NIGHT

Ichabod is startled awake, frightened, sweating.

47 INT. VAN TASSEL HOUSE, KITCHEN—NIGHT

Ichabod enters with a lantern and his Ledger. He sits, studies notes, then notices a light down the hall.

48 INT. VAN TASSEL HOUSE, SEWING ROOM—NIGHT

Ichabod enters. Opposite an elaborate **LOOM**, Katrina reads by candlelight.

She looks up, and self-consciously closes her book, which we see is a child's version of *The Knights of the Round Table*. She covers it on her lap.

ICHABOD

Oh . . . pardon my intrusion . . . I saw a light . . .

KATRINA

It is no intrusion . . . I come here to read when I am wakeful.

ICHABOD

To read books which you must hide . . .?

KATRINA

They were my mother's books . . . my father frowned at them then, and would frown at me now. He believes tales of romance caused the brain fever that killed my mother. She died two years ago come midwinter.

Ichabod nods.

ICHABOD

I saw it written in the front of the Bible.

KATRINA

The nurse who cared for her during her sickness is now
Lady Van Tassel.

ICHABOD

There was something else too. Why did no one think to mention
that Van Garretts are kith and kin to the Van Tassels?

KATRINA

Why, because there is hardly a household in Sleepy Hollow that is not
connected to every other by blood or marriage. I have more cousins
than fingers and toes to count them on.

A cock crows. Ichabod goes to the window to look at the edge of dawn.

ICHABOD

I see.

KATRINA

This land was Van Garrett Land, given to my father when I was in
swaddling clothes.

ICHABOD

Given by the dead Van Garrett?

KATRINA

(nods)
The Van Garretts were the richest family round these parts even then.
When my father brought us to Sleepy Hollow, Van Garrett set him up
with an acre and a broken-down cottage, and a dozen of Van Garrett
hens. My father prospered, and built us a new house. I owe my happi-
ness to him. I remember living poor in the cottage. Should I show you?

ICHABOD

Yes. I would like to see where you were as poor as I am.

Katrina stands up, revealing a Book that had been on the floor, hidden by her skirt. She picks up the
book and gives it to Ichabod.

KATRINA

Take this. It is my gift for you.

Ichabod looks at the title page: *A COMPENDIUM OF SPELLS, CHARMS AND DEVICES OF THE
SPIRIT WORLD*.

ICHABOD

(troubled)
But I have no use for . . .

KATRINA

Are you so certain of everything?

Ichabod sees that Katrina's name is written on the endpaper, and, in a different hand, her mother's name, "Elizabeth Van Tassel."

ICHABOD

It was your mother's . . . ?

KATRINA

Keep it close to your heart. It is sure protection against harm.

ICHABOD

(smiles)

Are you so certain of everything?

Their eyes meet and hold for a moment. Ichabod accepts the book by placing it on the desk.

49 EXT. FIELDS—DAY (EARLY MORNING)

Ichabod and Katrina make a pretty picture on horseback, riding slowly toward the cottage.

50 EXT. SLEEPY HOLLOW FARMLAND—DAY (EARLY MORNING)

Ichabod and Katrina, riding, come upon the ruin of a cottage. There is almost nothing left but the hearth and a part of a chimney.

Ichabod dismounts and helps Katrina down from her horse, taking her hand.

Before he lets go, she notices the little scars on his palm. She takes both his hands and looks at them.

KATRINA

These are strange . . . What are they . . . ?

ICHABOD

I wish I knew. I had them since I can
remember.

Katrina holds his hands a moment longer, their eyes meet, then she lets go
and "enters" the ruin.

Ichabod's attention is caught by a red Cardinal on a branch, like the bird he
had in New York.

He reflects a moment, then turns to watch Katrina crouching by the hearth.
She has put a flower in her hair.

KATRINA

I used to play by this hearth. It was my
first drawing school and my mother was
my teacher.

Unwittingly, Katrina is mimicking Ichabod's dream. She picks up a twig and
starts "drawing" on the hearth stone. Like Ichabod's mother in his dream.

Ichabod's blood runs cold but she is unaware of him. Then he notices that a few
small wildflowers are growing in the old fireplace. Ichabod feels short of breath,
he leans against the stones for support.

KATRINA (CONT'D)

Oh, look! I'd forgotten this!—see—carved
into the fire-back, the Archer!

Using her fingers she cleans off the dirt around a simple carving of a man
with a Bow and Arrow.

KATRINA (CONT'D)

This was from long before we lived here.

She turns to show Ichabod and notices him looking strange.

KATRINA (CONT'D)

Are you all right?

Ichabod nods, recovering, saying nothing.

Katrina is reassured. Suddenly her attention is caught, as Ichabod's was, by
the Cardinal bird.

KATRINA (CONT'D)

> (pointing)
> Oh, look! A Cardinal! My favorite! I would love to have a tame one,
> but I wouldn't have the heart to cage him.

Ichabod unslings his satchel.

ICHABOD

> Then I have something for you.

He has a **PAPER DISK** with a **BIRD** on one side and an **EMPTY CAGE** on the other, pierced by a looped string on which the disk can twist and spin. He demonstrates like a magician. This is the very Toy given to him by his Mother.

ICHABOD (CONT'D)

> A Cardinal on one side, and an empty cage.

Katrina watches intently. Ichabod spins the Disk.

ICHABOD (CONT'D)

And now . . .

The bird appears to be inside the cage.

Katrina is astonished and delighted.

KATRINA

You can do magic! Teach me!

ICHABOD

It is no magic. It is optics.

Ichabod gives her the Toy and shows her how to spin it.

ICHABOD (CONT'D)

Separate pictures which become one picture in the spinning . . .
Like the truth which I must spin here . . .

Katrina spins the disk, the bird appears in the cage.

52 EXT. PHILIPSE HOUSE—NIGHT

A **MOVING POV** is checking out the Village House. Through lighted windows, figures of Men are seen pacing, apparently arguing.

Philipse is packing his bags, moving out . . . while three Men, Steenwyck, Doctor Lancaster and Hardenbrook, are in agitated conference. Their raised voices make an undecipherable hubbub. The **POV's** horse makes a horsey snuffling sound. Is it Daredevil?

Steenwyck comes right to the window as if he has seen something . . . but he merely closes the shutters.

The **REVERSE** shows that it is Ichabod who has been spying.

Ichabod backs off and mounts Gunpowder, looking thoughtful, then determined.

53 EXT. ROAD OUTSIDE VILLAGE—NIGHT

A Mounted Man is approaching on a heavily loaded Pack Horse . . . Philipse making his getaway from Sleepy Hollow. As he reaches the foreground, Ichabod on Gunpowder intercepts him, grabbing the bridle of the Pack Horse.

PHILIPSE

What are you doing? Let go!

ICHABOD

What are you running from, Magistrate Philipse?

PHILIPSE

Damn you, Crane—

ICHABOD

You'll raise the village.

Philipse calms down.

ICHABOD (CONT'D)

You had a mind to help me.

PHILIPSE

Yes—and I put myself in mortal dread of . . .

ICHABOD

Of . . . what?

PHILIPSE

Powers against which there is no defense.

ICHABOD

How did you know the widow was expecting a child?

PHILIPSE

She told me.

ICHABOD

Then I deduce you are the father.

PHILIPSE

I hope your deductions serve you better in your contest
against the Hessian. I am not the father.

ICHABOD

Did she tell you the name of the child's father?

PHILIPSE

Yes—she did. She came to me for advice—as the town magistrate—

Ichabod hears sounds . . . of sheep in agitation at some distance but he holds Philipse to his story.

PHILIPSE (CONT'D)

—to protect the rights of her child. I was bound by my oath of office to
keep the secret—

ICHABOD

Do you believe the father killed her?

PHILIPSE

(stares at him in surprise)
The Horseman killed her!—You damn fool, do you suppose the
Horseman stops to impregnate our women?

ICHABOD

The Horseman? How often do I have to tell you there is no Horseman!
There never was a Horseman!—and there never will be a Horseman!

Ichabod grabs him fiercely, pulling on the amulet Philipse wears around his neck.

PHILIPSE

Let go!—it is my talisman that protects me from the Horseman!

ICHABOD

You a magistrate!—and your head full of such nonsense! Now tell me the name of—

A flock of sheep comes streaming and bleating across the path.

The horses go crazy, **BRAYING** and rearing. A **SOUND** is **HEARD**, distant: **THUNDERING HOOFBEATS**. Wind kicks up.

Philipse looks to the forest. A **FLOCK** of **BIRDS** alights.

PHILIPSE

Oh my . . . oh my oh my oh my . . .

Philipse runs away. **HOOFBEATS LOUDER**, **CLOSER**. Ichabod faces the forest.

The forest explodes open, foliage bending to make way as the **HEADLESS HORSEMAN** gallops into view atop **DAREDEVIL**.

Ichabod's stunned. He looks down to draw his flintlock pistol, but the Horseman **ROARS** by before he can raise it—a blast of air knocks Ichabod off his horse.

After this, everything happens very quickly—

The Horseman chases Philipse.

Philipse looks over his shoulder.

The Horseman draws his sword.

Philipse gathers his courage and stops, turning. He raises his iron key talisman before him. The Horseman is closing . . .

ICHABOD

Philipse!

Philipse holds the talisman up, trying to be fearless. The Horseman swings his sword upon the talisman—**CLANK** . . .

Philipse's severed head spins. His body falls and folds.

The two pieces of Philipse's Talisman, an Iron Key, fly through the air, toward Ichabod, who has only just managed to find his feet and find his fallen pistol.

The Horseman turns Daredevil in a wide circle . . .

Daredevil completes the turn, letting out a **SCREECHY CRY** as the Horseman rides straight toward Ichabod . . .

Before Ichabod has time to take aim, the Horseman is upon him and past him!—heading toward Philipse's corpse . . . leans effortlessly to skewer Philipse's head with his sword.

With the head as his prize, the Horseman races away.

Ichabod turns, watches the Horseman head to the forest.

Ichabod stands, stricken. He faints.

54 INT. VAN TASSEL HOUSE, ICHABOD'S BEDROOM—DAY

Ichabod gasps awake. A **KNOCKING** is **HEARD**.

BALTUS'S VOICE (O.S.)

Constable Crane . . . ?

Ichabod looks at his hand balled into a fist. He opens his hand—holds **BOTH HALVES** of **PHILIPSE'S IRON KEY TALISMAN.**

55 INT. VAN TASSEL HOUSE, UPSTAIRS HALL 3RD FLOOR—DAY

Young Masbath is seated by Ichabod's closed door. Katrina is backing up Baltus, who knocks again.

> **BALTUS**
> Has he not come out at all?

Young Masbath shakes his head.

56 INT. VAN TASSEL HOUSE, ICHABOD'S ROOM—DAY

Baltus enters. Katrina and Masbath follow him, cautiously, "visiting the sick."
Ichabod sits up in bed, stunned, spaced out.

> **ICHABOD**
> It was a Headless Horseman!

> **BALTUS**
> You must not excite yourself.

> **ICHABOD**
> But it was a Headless Horseman!

Who would wish evil

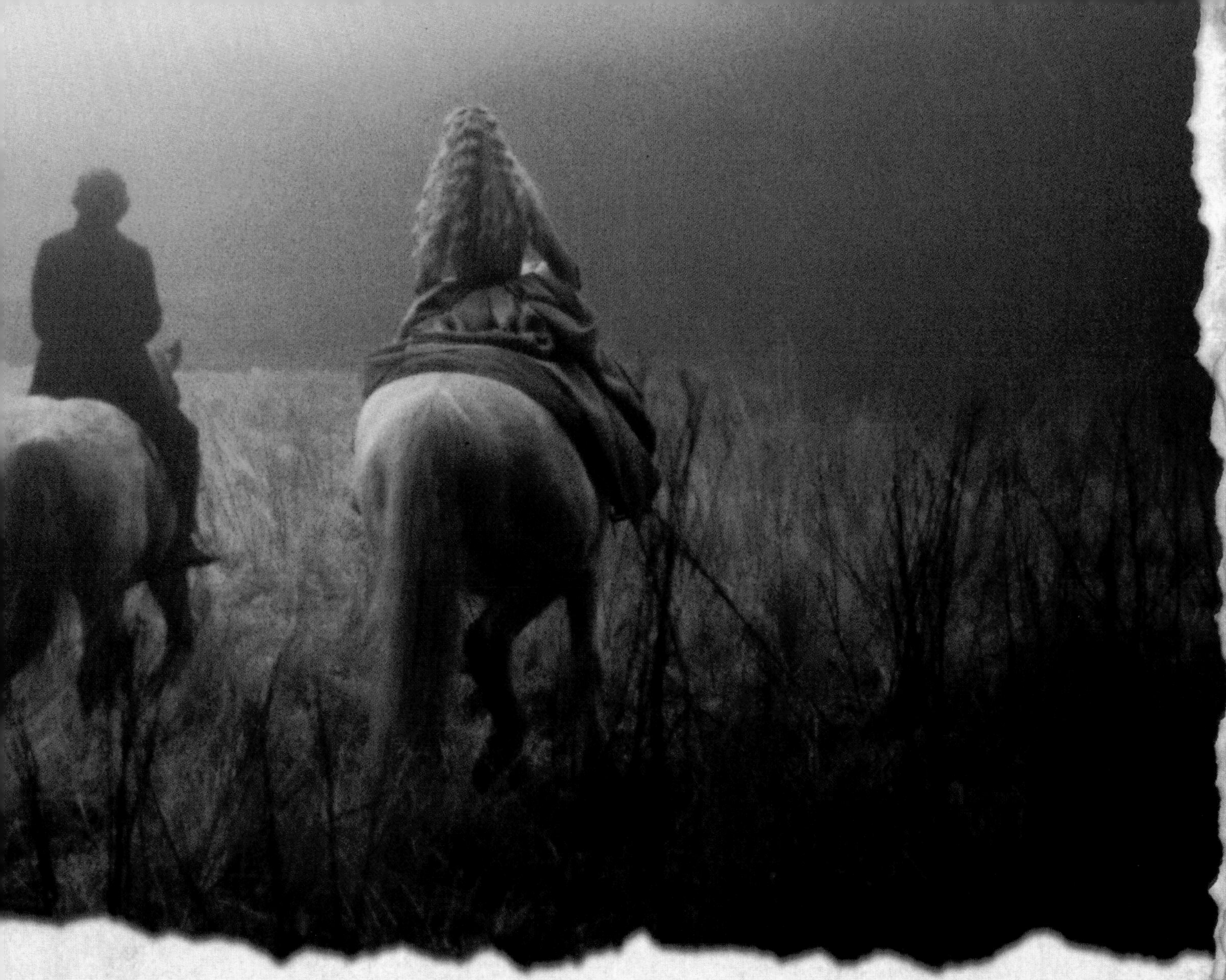

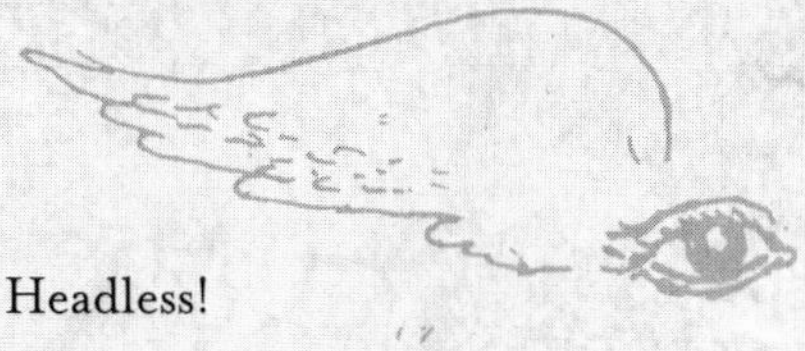

BALTUS

Of course it was.

ICHABOD

No, you must believe me, it was a Horseman! A dead one! Headless!

BALTUS

I know, I know . . .

ICHABOD

You don't know because you weren't there! But it's all true!

BALTUS

Of course it is. I told you! Everyone told you!

ICHABOD

(wildly)

I saw him!

His eyes roll up and he faints. Katrina and Masbath look helplessly at each other.

to befall me?

YOUNG MASBATH
I suppose it's back to the City, then.

Katrina's reaction is mixed—glad that Ichabod will be safe, sorry if he leaves.

57 ICHABOD'S DREAM—FOREST—DAY

A **MILLION WHITE MILKWEED SEEDLINGS** are floating in sunlight. Young Ichabod's laughter is heard.

Now we see that his Mother is blowing the seedlings for his delight. She gives him a milkweed pod and shows him how to do it for himself. Ichabod breaks the pod and releases another million. But when he looks around to share the delight, his Mother has gone . . . and he sees her disappearing among the trees. He goes to follow her.

58 ICHABOD'S DREAM—FOREST GLADE—DAY

Ichabod can't see his Mother anywhere . . .

Then he sees her standing in the middle of a **CIRCLE OF BEAUTIFUL TOADSTOOLS/MUSHROOMS** growing in the Glade.

Ichabod watches as his Mother turns inside the Mushroom Circle, almost dancing. He smiles. Then he sees his Mother stoop to pick a mushroom. She eats it. She looks happy. She drops a small piece of the mushroom.

Ichabod sees it fall.

He runs forward and picks it up before she sees him. Ichabod eats it. His Mother sees him, takes his hands in hers and dances him around in a circle.

As Ichabod whizzes around laughing, his **POV** becomes the Encircling Trees whizzing around, and suddenly he seems to be surrounded by Menacing Headless Figures dressed all in black.

Ichabod falls over dizzy and when he looks up he sees that the Headless Figures have become his Father, watching his Mother heedlessly dancing, his face like thunder. His Mother has loosened her clothes and is virtually barebreasted.

His Father's eyes begin to glow like live coals as Ichabod cowers away from him.

59 ICHABOD'S DREAM—ICHABOD'S HOUSE—NIGHT

Ichabod's eyes are spying . . . through a crack in the kitchen door.

When we see him properly, he is wearing a nightshirt. Then we see his **POV**, into the kitchen.

60 ICHABOD'S DREAM—YOUNG ICHABOD'S KITCHEN—NIGHT

Mother is seated, her head down. Father paces, chastising Mother angrily, his fist balled up in rage.

Father continues berating Mother. He picks up his Bible off the table, waving it, then grabs Mother by the shoulders, forcing her to the floor . . .

Father forces Mother to her knees. Mother is afraid, clasping her hands in front of her as Father forces her to pray. Father starts reading from the Bible. In Ichabod's dream, this is the same Bible from Baltus's house.

61 ICHABOD'S DREAM—YOUNG ICHABOD'S STAIRWELL—NIGHT

Ichabod watches, afraid. He backs away, returning upstairs.

62 ICHABOD'S DREAM—YOUNG ICHABOD'S BEDROOM—NIGHT

A window is thrown **CRASHING** open, **THUNDER BOOMING** . . . Young Ichabod sits up in his bed. He goes to close the window, **RAIN** pouring in. He looks down . . .

63 ICHABOD'S DREAM—EXT. YOUNG ICHABOD'S HOUSE—NIGHT

Below, in front of the home, a **MAN** drags Mother toward a **COACH**. **TWO MEN** stand watching, faces hidden under hat brims. Mother looks back, eyes pleading, struggling . . .

Mother looks up to Young Ichabod.

The **TWO MEN** look up to Young Ichabod: one is Father, and the **THIRD MAN** is a Cotton Mather-ish man with a villainous face.

Young Ichabod reaches helplessly toward Mother.

Mother is forced into the coach.

The Third Man speaks to Father, then walks to the coach. He gets onto the coach as the coach starts away.

Father watches, rain flowing down his stony features. **LIGHTNING FLASHES** . . . And we see the family Cat watching with glowing eyes.

64 INT. VAN TASSEL HOUSE—DAY

Ichabod's eyes as he opens them. He wakes, breathing heavily.

After a beat, he flings back the bedclothes and springs out of bed, energized by a new determination.

65 INT. VAN TASSEL HOUSE, DOWNSTAIRS—DAY

Baltus, Steenwyck, Doctor Lancaster and Notary Hardenbrook are having another meeting, this time with Lady Van Tassel and Katrina on hand with the drinks.

> **BALTUS**
> Right—this time I'll go to New York myself and I won't be fobbed off
> with an amateur deductor.

> **HARDENBROOK**
> (correcting him)
> Detector.

> **STEENWYCK**
> (correcting)
> Deductive.

> **DOCTOR LANCASTER**
> (doubting)
> No . . . no . . .

BALTUS
(rising above it)
An amateur sleuth! This time it's a magistrate that's dead, and—

The door is flung open without ceremony.

It's Ichabod ready for action, transformed, raring to go—with Young Masbath round-eyed just behind him.

ICHABOD
Gentlemen!—I need able men, to go with me to the Western Woods.
Who will be the first to volunteer?

BALTUS
You . . . ? We thought you'd shot your bolt . . .

ICHABOD
A setback, merely.
And yet, a step forward too—we now know who has done these terrible—

STEENWYCK
You now know, we already knew—

ICHABOD
(high on it)
Quite so—and now it seems fate has chosen me to make my name in a
case without parallel in the annals of crime—in short, to pit myself
against a murdering ghost.

KATRINA
(fearful for him)
No, Ichabod—Constable—

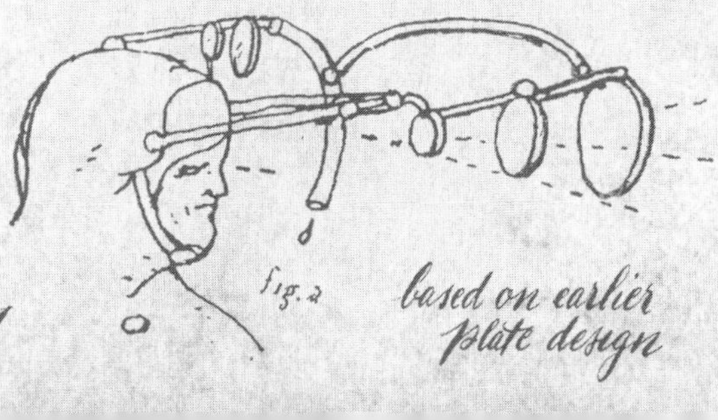

*the optics of
forensic detection* →

fig. 2

*based on earlier
plate design*

73

> **LADY VAN TASSEL**
> (smiles)
> Do you intend to arrest him? Or impound his horse . . . ?

The Men chuckle indulgently.

> **ICHABOD**
> Neither. To put an end to the killing. To discover the cause
> and remove it. Who's with me?

No one.

67 EXT. WESTERN WOODS—DAY

No one, indeed . . . Ichabod and Young Masbath ride alone . . . their horses loaded up for
the expedition.

Dark, gnarled and creepy woods. Ichabod and Young Masbath move through. **SOUND OF BIRDS** etc.

> **ICHABOD**
> The Van Garretts, the Widow Winship . . . your father, Jonathan
> Masbath . . . and now Philipse . . . Something must connect them.
> Can you think?

> **YOUNG MASBATH**
> (shakes his head)
> We had no dealings with the magistrate that I know of . . .

> **ICHABOD**
> And the widow? Your father knew her?

                    YOUNG MASBATH
     (shrugs)
Everyone knew Widow Winship.

                        ICHABOD
In a manner of speaking, I trust.

                    YOUNG MASBATH
She would bring old Mr. Van Garrett a basket of eggs many a day.

                        ICHABOD
Did your father have dealings with the Van Garretts?

                    YOUNG MASBATH
     (surprised)
He worked for them, we lived in the coach house.

Ichabod halts his horse, surprised.

                YOUNG MASBATH (CONT'D)
It's nothing—there were many servants . . . all dismissed now,
of course.
     (beat—they ride on)
But there was something happened one night, a week before the
murder. An argument upstairs between father and son, and my
father was later sent for by Mr. Van Garrett.

                        ICHABOD
An argument between father and son?
     (to himself, thoughtfully)
After which, the elder Van Garrett summoned his servant, Masbath . . .

Young Masbath halts his horse and looks around.

                    YOUNG MASBATH
Listen.

                        ICHABOD
I hear nothing.

                    YOUNG MASBATH
Nor I—no birds—no crickets—

Everything has gone quiet.

                YOUNG MASBATH (CONT'D)
—it's all gone so quiet . . .

*Chemical test results yielded an almost
neglible trace of blood!*

Ichabod notes this nervously.

> **ICHABOD**
> You're right!

He gees up the horses. They break into a gallop. **A MOVING POV** watches them gallop by.

68 EXT. WESTERN WOODS AND CAVE ENTRANCE—DAY

Ichabod and Masbath reach a hill crest. They stop, uneasy.

BELOW, there is a **CAVE** with a rock archway. An ill-fitting **DOOR** covers the mouth. The chimney spews smoke.

Ichabod and Masbath share a fearful look.

ELSEWHERE, SOMEONE WATCHES . . . **A MOVING POV WATCHES** Ichabod and Masbath as they ride to the cave, **FOLLOWING** . . .

Ichabod and Young Masbath dismount, tying their horses, then heading to the cave. They arrive at the cave door. Ichabod hesitantly **KNOCKS**.

69 INT. CAVE HOME—DAY

The door is ajar . . . Ichabod and Young Masbath step in . . . Walls are hung with **SKINS** and **SKELETONS**. Across the cave, a **CRONE** sits facing away, motionless.

Ichabod and Young Masbath look to each other, fearful.

ICHABOD

Pardon my intrusion . . .

The Crone, with gray hair and gray features, sits disinterested. Behind, Ichabod edges slowly forward . . .

CRONE

You are from the Hollow?

ICHABOD

In a way, yes. I, um . . .

Ichabod is distracted by gourd **BOWLS** of **DEAD INSECTS**, **LEAVES** and **ACORNS** . . . **KNIVES**, **SCISSORS** and **YELLOWED BONES**.

ICHABOD (CONT'D)

I should like to say . . . um . . . I make no assumptions about
your occupation, no, your ways, witch—which—which are nothing
to me . . . um . . . whatever you are, each to his own—um—

The Crone places something on a table beside her . . . a **DEAD BIRD**, a bright red cardinal.

Ichabod backs away, but Masbath comes to stand beside him.

YOUNG MASBATH

Do you know of the Horseman, ma'am . . . ? The Hessian.

The Crone draws her finger across her neck.

YOUNG MASBATH (CONT'D)

That'll be him, miss.

Around her neck is a cord on which is threaded a carved stone, a mystic bauble.
Ichabod notices it. The Crone stands, faces them, tall . . . points to Ichabod.

CRONE

You, follow with me.
    (to Young Masbath)
Go out, child. Keep away. No matter what you hear, keep away.

She takes a candle and heads deeper into the cave . . .

70 INT. CAVE HOME, LOWER CAVE—DAY

The Crone enters through a passage. Ichabod follows, terrified, bent under the low ceiling.

ICHABOD

Um . . . what might he hear that he must keep away from . . . ?

CRONE

Sit there.

Ichabod sits on a crooked stool. The Crone kneels with her back to him, grasps two **METAL CUFFS**
with chains attached, slides these onto her wrists, testing them . . .

CRONE (CONT'D)

He rides, to the Hollow and back. I hear him. I smell the blood
on him.

ICHABOD

Do . . . do you? Well . . . I'm here to find him and . . . er . . .
make him stop . . .

CRONE

You want to see into the netherworld . . . I can show you . . .

The Crone gathers **STRAW** in a pile on the floor, then gathers bowls, putting **GRASS** and **POWDER** on the pile, **WITHERING** over it. She takes a **JAR** from a table.

ICHABOD

What . . . what are you doing?

The Crone shakes one jar, pulls the lid off and upends it. A **BABY BAT** squirms, dazed. The Crone grips the bat, uses a knife to cut off its head, soaks the straw with blood.

CRONE

Do not move or speak. When the other comes,
I will hold him.

Using her candle, the Crone lights the straw pile.

ICHABOD

The other . . . ?

CRONE

Silence.
    (bends to inhale smoke)
He comes now.

Ichabod would like to leave now.

71 EXT. CAVE HOME—DAY

Young Masbath waits. **WIND** picks up, kicking leaves, sending them in swirls. Masbath holds himself against the chill.

72 INT. CAVE HOME, LOWER CAVE—DAY

The Crone slumps face forward to the floor, suddenly immobile, still with her back to Ichabod. **WIND HOWLS** through a hole/window.

Ichabod looks around, uncertain, stands.

> ICHABOD
> Excuse me . . . ma'am . . . ?

The Crone remains motionless. The **WIND** intensifies. Candles blow out. Ichabod inches closer . . .

> ICHABOD (CONT'D)
> Do you hear me . . . ?

73 INT. CAVE HOME, LOWER CAVE—DAY

The Crone suddenly jumps erect, spinning—a half-human, half-demon **CREATURE**, black clawed hands reaching . . .

Ichabod cries out, leaping backward . . .

CHAINS on the restraining **CUFFS** around the creature's hands go taut, yanking the creature back.

Ichabod **KNOCKS** over a table of bones, hits the floor. The creature is chained, but still wants Ichabod. It **SHRIEKS**.

The creature's face still seethes from transformation.

> CREATURE/CRONE
> You seek the warrior bathed in blood . . . the Headless
> Horseman . . .

Ichabod scrambles back as far as possible. The creature claws the rock floor, yearning.

> CREATURE/CRONE (CONT'D)
> Follow the Indian trail to where the sun dies. Follow to the Tree
> of the Dead . . .

The creature yanks, testing the chains. Behind, the **BOLT** holding the chains slips . . . the **WALL CRACKS** a little.

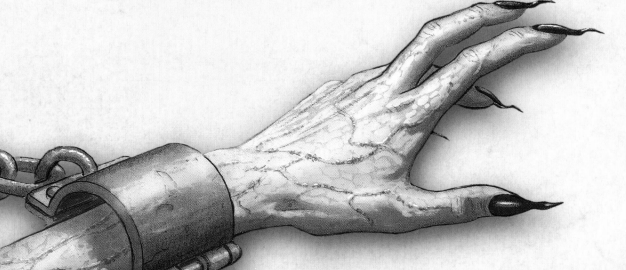

CREATURE/CRONE (CONT'D)

Climb down to the Horseman's resting place. Do you hear . . . ?

Ichabod nods, quaking, aghast. He glances to the exit.

The chain bolt gives more . . . coming loose . . .

Ichabod flees toward the door. The creature **HOWLS**, leaping . . . the chain bolt **BREAKS** . . .

Ichabod cries out as he is **TACKLED** to the floor . . .

74 INT. CAVE HOME, LOWER CAVE—DAY

It is only the **CRONE** lying on him; she has returned to human form, semiconscious. Ichabod desperately shoves her off . . .

75 EXT. CAVE HOME—DAY

Ichabod sprints out from the cave, past Young Masbath.

ICHABOD

We are leaving.

YOUNG MASBATH

What happened?

ICHABOD

We are leaving now.

Ichabod scrambles onto Gunpowder, riding, glancing back. Young Masbath follows.

76 EXT. WESTERN WOODS AREA TWO, FARTHER ON—LATER DAY

Ichabod and Young Masbath ride side by side.

ICHABOD

(quoting)
"Take the Indian trail . . . To the Tree of the Dead . . ."

YOUNG MASBATH

How will we recognize it?

ICHABOD

Without difficulty I rather fear. And "Climb down to the Horseman's resting place . . ." she said.

YOUNG MASBATH

His . . . camp?

ICHABOD

His grave.

A **SNAPPING BRANCH** is **HEARD**. Ichabod turns to look back . . .

ICHABOD (CONT'D)

(whispers to Masbath)
Quicken pace.

Ichabod rides faster. Young Masbath keeps up . . .

FARTHER ON, they charge over a hill. Ichabod halts Gunpowder, climbs clumsily off, handing the reins to Masbath.

> ICHABOD (CONT'D)
>
> Ride on.

Young Masbath obeys. Ichabod takes out his pistol and wades into forest growth, backtracking . . .

77 EXT. WESTERN WOODS AREA THREE—DAY

INSIDE THE FOREST, Ichabod moves through **UNDERBRUSH**, keeping low. A **HORSE** is **HEARD SNORTING**.

Ichabod forges on, pushes through branches, fearful . . .

He comes up behind a **FIGURE IN A GRAY CLOAK** on horseback, raising his pistol, cocking the hammer . . .

> ICHABOD
>
> Halt and turn! I have a pistol aimed.

The **FIGURE** stops, pushes off the cloak hood. It is Katrina.

> KATRINA
>
> It is me.

> ICHABOD
> (lowers gun, shaken)
> Katrina . . . I might have killed you. Why have you come?

> KATRINA
> Because no one else would go with you.

She smiles a little. Ichabod is heartened.

> ICHABOD
> I am now twice the man.

Ichabod takes her hand.

> ICHABOD (CONT'D)
> It is your white magic.

She is about to turn this moment into a kiss—but . . .

> YOUNG MASBATH (O.S.)
> Pardon my intrusion . . .

Ichabod and Katrina look to see Masbath has backtracked.

> YOUNG MASBATH
> I think you'd better come and look at this . . .

Ichabod and Katrina move to follow Young Masbath.

78 EXT. WESTERN WOODS, TREE OF THE DEAD—DUSK

Ichabod, Masbath and Katrina come into a clearing, slowing their horses . . . looking up in wonder at . . .

The monstrously huge **TREE OF THE DEAD**, at the clearing's center.

Its branches reach far and wide, knotted and gross, like agony captured in wood sculpture.

> YOUNG MASBATH
> The Tree of the Dead.

> KATRINA
> It does announce itself.

Ichabod dismounts, crossing a line beyond which grass and weeds will not grow. Young Masbath and Katrina dismount behind. They all walk toward the tree . . .

Ichabod stares up into the endless, dead canopy of branches.

There's a **VERTICAL WOUND** in the bark, like a terrible suture, now healed and scarred. Ichabod approaches . . .

He feels the mushy scar, picking at its scabs till sap begins to run Red Sap. Ichabod fingers it, sniffs it.

> ICHABOD
> Blood.

> KATRINA
> The tree bleeds? How can it be?

Ichabod goes to where Katrina and Masbath wait with the horses, digs in a saddle bag for a hand **AXE**.

> **YOUNG MASBATH**
>
> What is it?

> **ICHABOD**
>
> Stay here.

At the trunk, Ichabod thumps the flat end of the axe against the suture. It sounds hollow. He begins to **CHOP** . . .

He **CHOPS** into the suture . . . pulls away loose bark. The tree drips more blood and a goo. Ichabod uses both hands on the axe to hack at the festering suture.

> **KATRINA**
>
> What are you doing?

> **ICHABOD**
>
> Just . . . keep where you are.

Young Masbath moves closer. Ichabod keeps **CHOPPING**, then grips a large, loose flap, trying to pull it away. It's not easy. Ichabod struggles.

Katrina follows Young Masbath's slow advance.

Ichabod's pulling—the flap suddenly gives, revealing a blood-soaked, wide-eyed, gap-mouthed **HUMAN HEAD**.

Ichabod recoils. Behind him, Katrina stifles a scream.

Ichabod backs off, back of his hand to his mouth.

It is **PHILIPSE'S HEAD**, hanging off the trunk flap, held by roots grown around and into the flesh.

FOUR other **SEVERED, DECAYING HEADS** are held by ingrown roots within the dewy innards.

One of the heads is Jonathan Masbath's. Before Young Masbath sees it, Katrina hides his face in her bosom and comforts him.

> **KATRINA**
>
> My God . . .

> **ICHABOD**
>
> He . . . he tries to take the heads
> back with him. They will not pass . . .

> **KATRINA**
>
> We must leave this place.

Ichabod looks to the branches towering above.

> **ICHABOD**
>
> This is . . . a gateway, between
> two worlds . . .

Ichabod studies the ground, circling the trunk . . . Around the other side, Ichabod gets to his knees . . .

He's found the **HORSEMAN'S SWORD**: the grave marker, jutting out from the ground, rusted twenty years' worth, gripped by the tree trunk and vines.

> ICHABOD (CONT'D)
> (touching the ground)
> Climb down to the Horseman's resting place . . .
> (looks to Masbath)
> Bring the shovel.

Now he sees Katrina hugging the boy.

> ICHABOD (CONT'D)
> Forgive me . . . I . . .

Young Masbath courageously recovers himself, wiping his eyes and nose on the back of his sleeve.

> YOUNG MASBATH
> Yes, sir—the shovel . . . Two shovels and the rifle, I suggest.

79 EXT. WESTERN WOODS, TREE OF THE DEAD—DUSK

Lantern light.

Young Masbath's crouched, rifle across his knees. He watches the tree, looking up . . .

High branches swarm with **BATS**.

Behind Masbath, Ichabod and Katrina dig up the **SHALLOW GRAVE**.

> KATRINA
> This ground has been disturbed, the soil is loose.

Ichabod throws down his Shovel.

Young Masbath comes to the grave. Ichabod pulls at thick **BURLAP CLOTH** heavy with dirt . . . straining as it comes away . . .

Ichabod drops the burlap, looking down, disbelieving . . .

> ICHABOD
> Look . . . !

WE SEE: Roots have gripped the **HORSEMAN'S BONES** and tattered uniform. The skeleton is all there—except the skull.

> KATRINA
> The skull is gone. What does it mean?

Ichabod jumps out from the grave, snapping his fingers.

> ICHABOD
> (energized)
> It means, my dear Miss Van Tassel, it means—yes! What exactly does it mean?—It means, unless I am much mistaken . . . it definitely means something—what that something is, only time will tell! But I sense that we are very close to the answer here, if only we had one more clue . . .

Ichabod is unaware that the ground is writhing around him.

> KATRINA (O.S.)
>
> Ichabod . . . !

Ichabod turns, looks . . .

Katrina and Young Masbath back away, because . . . the **ROOTS** in the grave are **ALIVE**, entwining around remains.

Ichabod spins to the twisted tree . . .

The vertical **SUTURE SEETHES**, pulling inward . . . sucking Philipse's head back in and closing, bubbling.

Ichabod bounds over the grave dirt pile, hastening Katrina and Young Masbath along as he flees across the field.

At the tree, the suture swells.

Ichabod, Katrina and Young Masbath pass where their freaking horses are tied to a fallen trunk, heading for cover.

A **RUMBLING** is **HEARD** from the tree. It's wound suddenly **BURSTS** wide, spitting smoldering cinders.

At the tree line, Ichabod, Katrina and Young Masbath take cover, looking back.

80 EXT. WESTERN WOODS TREE OF THE DEAD (EFFECT)—DUSK

From the tree wound, a glow **BRIGHTENS** . . . till suddenly the Headless Horseman and Daredevil **EXPLODE** into existence . . . They hit the ground running.

81 EXT. WESTERN WOODS TREE OF THE DEAD—DUSK

Ichabod watches the Horseman ride away, bolts of **LIGHTNING STRIKING** the **GROUND BEHIND**.

The Horseman disappears into the forest.

> ICHABOD
>
> (to Masbath)
> Did you see that?!
> (recovering)
> Take Katrina home!

Ichabod runs toward the horses.

> YOUNG MASBATH
>
> Constable!

82 EXT. WESTERN WOODS AREA TWO—NIGHT

The Horseman rips past on Daredevil . . .

83 EXT. BEHIND IN WESTERN WOODS AREA
THREE—NIGHT

Ichabod rides as fast as Gunpowder is able . . .

84 EXT. WESTERN WOODS AREA TWO, FARTHER ON—NIGHT

Trees are silhouetted against the sky. As Daredevil's **HOOFBEATS** get **LOUDER**, branches bend like arms and fingers yearning to touch. As **HOOFBEATS ROAR PAST**, the trees relax.

85 EXT. WESTERN WOODS AREA TWO, FARTHER ON—NIGHT

Ichabod ducks under foliage as he pursues. He sees . . .

Through the forest ahead: the **SKY'S LIT UP**. Distant fire.

86 EXT. WESTERN WOODS, CAVE HOME—NIGHT

The Crone's **CAVE** vomits **FLAME**.

Ichabod arrives on Gunpowder, horrified, struggling for control as Gunpowder rears, trying to see through **BLACK SMOKE** . . .

Embers swirl everywhere. Ichabod dismounts, moving closer to the cave . . . suddenly he **SLIPS** . . .

Ichabod falls down a bloody rock, landing very close to the **CRONE'S HEADLESS BODY**. Ichabod recoils, crawling away, looking to the carnage in terror . . .

The corpse lies near the cave entrance. The jagged skin of the neck wound still bleeds. The ground and dead leaves around the corpse are thick with **BLOOD**. Ichabod crawls back to the Crone, terrified . . . because he has seen a **CLUE**.

The cord around the Crone's neck has been cut and the Carved Bauble is missing (along with the Crone's head.)

Ichabod hears a Horse neighing in the trees . . . and the sound of the horse crashing through the undergrowth, departing . . . but he can see nothing.

87 EXT. FOREST—NIGHT

Brom, Theodore and Glen are on patrol—Brom with his new rifle. They can hear the same horse crashing invisibly through branches, the sound of hooves. They can't tell where the sound is coming from. They look around nervously.

BROM

Split up! He won't get away.

The three of them gallop off in three directions.

When they clear the frame there is a sound of deep rumbling, the sound we heard before Jonathan Masbath was murdered.

88 INT. KILLIAN'S HOME, KITCHEN—NIGHT

Small home. Killian, Thomas and **BETH**, Killian's wife, have finished supper. Beth clears plates as Killian picks his teeth with a knife.

The same rumbling sound is faintly heard.

The glasses on the table shiver audibly. Killian notices. Then the phenomenon stops. Killian continues picking his teeth.

Thomas gets down from his chair. He goes to the fireplace to light a tallow wick, which he takes to the next room.

89 INT. KILLIAN'S HOME, WHITE ROOM—NIGHT

Thomas plops on the floor and lights his **MAGIC LANTERN**: a lantern with an outer sleeve of glass painted with **SILHOUETTES** of **LIONS** and **MONSTERS**.

Thomas turns the lantern and looks to the walls where the creatures' **SHADOWS** are cast.

He roars for them, imagining them real and having a grand time.

90 INT. KILLIAN'S HOME, KITCHEN—NIGHT

Beth comes for more dishes.

> **BETH**
> Don't pick teeth. You teach Thomas bad habits.

Killian pulls her to him, playful.

> **KILLIAN**
> I am a bad habit. There's nothing for it.

> **BETH**
> (kisses him)
> Oh, isn't there.

91 EXT. FOREST—NIGHT

A black horse runs, hooves pounding the ground.

THUNDER is **HEARD**. The horse stops . . . it is Brom's horse, with Brom riding. Brom looks skyward.

All around, the **WIND HALTS**. A **DEAD SILENCE** falls. Distant **HOOFBEATS** can be **HEARD**.

Brom takes his long rifle from his shoulder, rides . . .

92 INT. KILLIAN'S HOME, KITCHEN—NIGHT

Behind Killian, **MANTELPIECE STONES** pulse, breathing. Demonic faces form, then disappear. **WIND HOWLS.**

93 INT. KILLIAN'S HOME, WHITE ROOM—NIGHT

Thomas continues his fun, shadow animals circling him. Beth enters, looking at Thomas, smiling.

The magic lantern suddenly stops spinning. Shadow creatures freeze. Beth looks up, noticing the **FEROCITY** of the **WIND.** The smile leaves her face.

94 INT. KILLIAN'S HOME, KITCHEN—NIGHT

The **ENTIRE HOUSE CREAKS.** Killian stands, looking up. The **HOUSE CREAKS** again, then suddenly the **WIND CEASES.** Silence.

KILLIAN

Beth . . .

95 INT. KILLIAN'S HOME, WHITE ROOM—NIGHT

Beth picks up Thomas. The magic lantern shadow creatures begin spinning anew, quickly, around and around.

96 INT. KILLIAN'S HOME, KITCHEN—NIGHT

With a **ROAR**, the fire flares. Killian looks . . . In the leaping flames he seems to see—as we also seem to see—the **ILLUSION OF DEMONIC FACES** molded out of flames.

Behind Killian, the **DOOR SPLINTERS INWARD**. The Horseman steps in, a battle axe in each hand. **WIND BLASTS** . . .

The **DOOR** to the other room **SLAMS**. Killian grabs a chair and **HURLS** it . . .

The Horseman swings, **SMASHING** it aside.

> KILLIAN
>
> Beth . . . run!

97 INT. KILLIAN'S HOME, WHITE ROOM—NIGHT

Beth holds Thomas as she backs away from the closed door.

> KILLIAN (CONT'D; O.S.)
> (from kitchen)
> Get out!

98 INT. KILLIAN'S HOME, KITCHEN—NIGHT

Killian grabs an **IRON SKEWER** from the fireplace, **SWINGS** it to fend off a blow from the Horseman.

The Horseman **SWINGS** the other axe. Killian ducks. The axe **CRACKS** fireplace stone, throwing sparks.

Killian lunges, **JAMMING** the skewer into the Horseman . . . The skewer comes through the Horseman's back. The Horseman **SWIPES** with the flat of one axe—**POUNDS** Killian aside . . .

Killian hits the wall, **BASHING** his head. Hits the floor.

99 INT. KILLIAN'S HOME, WHITE ROOM—NIGHT

Beth kicks a carpet to reveal a **TRAP DOOR**.

100 INT. KILLIAN'S HOME, KITCHEN—NIGHT

The Horseman pulls the skewer out of his body, throws it. He goes to lift Killian by the hair with one hand, brings back the axe in the other hand . . .

101 INT. KILLIAN'S HOME, WHITE ROOM—NIGHT

At the trap door, Beth lowers Thomas to stairs leading to a **CRAWL SPACE** under the **GAPPED** floorboards. Thomas is crying.

> BETH
> Hush—hush—quiet as a mouse, now.

> THOMAS
> Mother . . .

> BETH
> You must hide . . .

Beth closes the trap door, frantically replacing the carpet. The room's door **FLIES OPEN** . . . the Horseman strides in, carrying Killian's severed head. Beth shrieks.

102 EXT. FOREST NEAR KILLIAN HOUSE—NIGHT

Brom, on his horse, hears Beth's shriek.

103 INT. KILLIAN'S HOME, CELLAR—NIGHT

Beth's **SCREAMS** are abruptly **CUT OFF**. Her **BODY** is **HEARD HITTING** the floor above. Thomas sees the shadow of Beth's head rolling across the gaps in the floorboards above him, coming to rest with her hair showing, hanging down in the gap. **FOOTSTEPS** are **HEARD** . . .

104 INT. KILLIAN'S HOME, WHITE ROOM—NIGHT

The Horseman's hands place Killian's and Beth's heads in a sack, cinching the sack shut.

105 INT. KILLIAN'S HOME, KITCHEN—NIGHT

The Headless Horseman enters, bends to retrieve the battle axe he left. He stands. Long, silent pause.

106 INT. KILLIAN'S HOME, CRAWL SPACE—NIGHT

Thomas cowers, trembling. **QUIET**.

107 INT. KILLIAN'S HOME, KITCHEN—NIGHT

The Horseman falls to his knees. He starts to **CHOP** at the floor with both axes. **CHOPPING**, **CHOPPING**, **CHOPPING** . . . making quick work of it . . .

108 INT. KILLIAN'S HOME, CRAWL SPACE—NIGHT

A hole appears as debris falls . . .

Thomas looks up. He tries to crawl away.

The Horseman's arm **SHOVES** through from above—grabbing Thomas and **YANKING** him up through the hole.

109 EXT. KILLIAN'S FARM, TOWN OUTSKIRTS—NIGHT

Brom rides from the forest.

Ahead, at Killian's house, among scattered homes on the outskirts of town, Daredevil rides up as the Headless Horseman walks out with his sack of heads. The Horseman ties the sack to his saddle and leaps up.

The Horseman ignores Brom. But Brom refuses to be ignored.

Brom puts his reins in his mouth, aims his rifle . . . **FIRING** . . .

BOOM—the slug blows the Horseman off Daredevil, **EXPLODING**. Daredevil keeps going. The Horseman's smoldering body is left "face down."

Brom halts his horse. He climbs down, pleased.

The Horseman moves.

Brom backs away, satisfaction diminishing.

The Horseman rises to his knees.

Brom falls to one knee, begins reloading. He fills the gun from his powder horn.

The Horseman stands, unsheathes his sword and turns. The blast has exposed rotten flesh and maggot-infested muscle.

Brom readies his ramrod, but there's no time. He rises, hefting his rifle, straight at the Horseman with a yell . . .

The Horseman is on him. Brom swings the rifle, blocking.

The battle is on, with Brom fending off the Horseman's sword with the rifle—**CLANK** . . . **CLANK** . . . **CLANK** . . .

ACROSS THE FIELD, Ichabod and Gunpowder arrive . . .

UP THE FIELD, the Horseman makes a backhanded swing, knocks Brom's rifle away, sends Brom to the ground . . .

The Horseman walks away from Brom. Ichabod sees this, registers it.

Brom pulls a knife and throws it.

The knife blade goes through the Horseman from back to front, like a spear thrust through a smoldering sack of rotten flesh. The Horseman pulls Brom's knife, blade first, from his chest and turns upon Brom.

Brom scrambles up, flees, running toward Killian's. The Horseman **THROWS** the knife . . .

THWAP—the knife imbeds in Brom's thigh.

The Horseman strides to Brom.

Ichabod closes in, pulling an unlit lantern off his saddle.

The Horseman changes his sword grip, blade down . . . plants one foot on Brom's back, raising his sword to skewer . . .

Ichabod arrives at full gallop—**SMASHES** the lantern into the Horseman—**KNOCKING** the Horseman off Brom.

IN THE DISTANCE, Theodore and Glen arrive on horseback. They halt where they are, watching.

Brom runs, limping to Killian's house, a goal in sight: **FARM IMPLEMENTS** propped there. Brom grabs **SCYTHES** with long curved blades, one in each hand.

The Horseman rises.

Ichabod leaps off Gunpowder, runs to Brom's side.

Once more, the Horseman turns away.

> BROM
>
> I'll get him!

Brom grabs Ichabod's pistol. Ichabod grabs Brom's pistol arm.

> ICHABOD
>
> Wait! Don't you see?—he's not after us!

Brom shakes himself free and—

FIRES—the bullet rips through the Horseman's stomach to reveal putrid innards.

The Horseman turns and strides back—no more nice guy!

> ICHABOD (CONT'D)
>
> He is now!

Brom throws the pistol at the Horseman.

Across the way, Theodore looks to Glenn, turns his horse and flees. Glenn follows Theodore away.

Brom steps up, scythes ready. He and the Horseman go at it—Brom blocks axe and sword, deflecting blows . . .

Ichabod grabs a long-handled SICKLE, circles them . . . SWINGS the sickle. The Horseman blocks.

The Horseman battles both men at once, catching blows . . . counting every strike, METAL RINGING.

Ichabod's sickle is knocked out of his hand.

Brom catches the Horseman's sword in one scythe, catches the axe handle in the other scythe . . .

The Horseman flatfoot KICKS Brom, sending him down.

Brom picks up Ichabod's sickle and SWINGS it . . .

The blade embeds in the Horseman down to the hilt.

> ICHABOD (CONT'D)
>
> Now you've annoyed him.

The Horseman drops his axe, grasps the sickle handle . . . The handle SLAMS Ichabod away . . .

Ichabod crawls, shaking off the blow. The Horseman staggers, trying to pull the blade from his body.

> ICHABOD (CONT'D)
>
> We cannot win this.

Brom yanks Ichabod to his feet and grabs his scythes.

As they flee, Ichabod grabs a wood-splitting AXE from the stump where it's imbedded.

Behind, the Horseman manages to extract the sickle, drops it.

103

Brom and Ichabod head toward the **COVERED BRIDGE** that leads across to the town square.

The Horseman strides after . . . retrieves his axe on the way.

110 EXT. TOWN SQUARE AND COVERED BRIDGE—NIGHT

Brom and Ichabod start across. Ichabod must help support Brom as Brom limps.

Behind, the Horseman picks up the pace, closing fast . . .

Inside the bridge, Ichabod and Brom are halfway across. **FOOTSTEPS** are **HEARD POUNDING.** Ichabod glances back . . .

The Horseman is not behind them. Ichabod and Brom look up. The **POUNDING FOOTSTEPS** are on the roof, passing over . . . !

Ahead, at the mouth of the covered bridge, the Horseman leaps down, spinning in midair, lands, crouched.

Ichabod and Brom halt. The Horseman rises.

Ichabod releases Brom and moves forward, gripping his wood axe in both hands, **SWINGING** the axe downward . . .

The Horseman swings his axe—**SPLINTERS** Ichabod's axe handle.

The Horseman, axe in one hand, sword in the other, turns upon Brom, and in pulling Brom aside out of the path of the sword, Ichabod receives a sword-thrust in the shoulder, which makes him scream out.

The Horseman lifts his sword arm, **THROWING** Ichabod and withdrawing the sword in one motion . . . Ichabod tumbles.

Brom moves forward with scythes. The Horseman sets upon him with incredible ferocity— battling Brom back, striking so hard and fast it's hard for Brom to keep blocking.

Ichabod tries to get up, but falls, looking up . . .

ICHABOD'S POV:

The Horseman **KNOCKS** one of Brom's scythes away, takes another **SWING**—sends Brom spinning in a spray of blood . . .

The Horseman stands over Brom's body, **CHOPPING** with his sword. Our **POINT OF VIEW** grows **BLURRY** . . .

A **BLURRY HORSEMAN** approaches the **POV**.

Ichabod is at the Horseman's mercy.

Then, another **ANGLE**—the Horseman ignores Ichabod, strides past him. Ichabod takes a step back and collapses.

FADE TO BLACK

111 INT. VAN TASSEL HOUSE, ICHABOD'S ROOM—NIGHT

Candlelight. Ichabod, shirtless, feverish, opens his eyes. The wound at the top of his chest is raw but with the edges sealed shut. Ichabod is on his bed. Doctor Lancaster bends over him. Baltus Van Tassel observes.

>   DOCTOR LANCASTER
> Remarkable. A wound like this should have killed him . . . but it
> needs no stitch and there's hardly loss of blood.

Baltus sees Ichabod's eyes open.

>   BALTUS
> He stirs.

Ichabod tries to rise, looking around, collapses in pain.

>   DOCTOR LANCASTER
> You must be still . . . the fever is on you.

>   ICHABOD
>   (weakly)
> Katrina . . .

112 INT. VAN TASSEL HOUSE, KITCHEN—NIGHT

A Woman is bent over the hearth, mumbling.

Then we see it is Katrina, mumbling over a boiling beaker of milk and green leaves. There is a dead crow on the hearth, with one foot chopped off and a sharp knife lying alongside.

>   KATRINA
>   (chanting, repeating the phrases)
> Nostradamus Mediamus, Milk Of Mercy In Media Nos Laudamas . . .

113 INT. VAN TASSEL HOUSE, ICHABOD'S ROOM—NIGHT

Katrina enters with the beaker of medicine. Baltus and Doctor Lancaster are bending over Ichabod, the Doctor trying to make Ichabod drink a livid green liquid from a shot glass.

DOCTOR LANCASTER

It will restore you.

Ichabod closes his lips tight and refuses the drink—he doesn't trust Lancaster. Katrina comes to the bedside with her beaker. Ichabod sees her. He is in pain, feverish.

ICHABOD

I . . . I . . . tried to stop Brom but . . .

Katrina soothes him.

KATRINA

Sssh . . . no one could have done more. Drink this down, it will make you sleep.

ICHABOD

The Horseman was not set to kill Brom . . . or me . . . If Brom had not attacked him . . .

BALTUS

Later. Rest now.

ICHABOD

I have discovered something.

Baltus and Doctor Lancaster glance at each other.

BALTUS

These are ravings . . .

ICHABOD

The Horseman does not kill for the sake of killing . . . he chooses his victims.

KATRINA

Drink . . .

She holds the beaker to Ichabod's lips. He drains it and falls back on the pillow, closing his eyes.

Baltus turns at a sound from the door.

Lady Van Tassel has entered quietly. She comes to him anxiously and grips his hand.

LADY VAN TASSEL

What is it, Baltus?

BALTUS

Nothing . . . nothing . . .
Don't be troubled, my love . . .

They hold hands lovingly, staring at Ichabod, who has fallen asleep.

114 ICHABOD'S DREAM—CHURCH—NIGHT

Empty church. Young Ichabod enters, carries a lantern past pews. He **HEARS** a **SOUND**, moving behind a pew to hide.

Ahead, across the church, a **RED DOOR** opens . . . Father and the villainous Third Man come out, shutting the door, speaking quietly. The Third Man holds a piece of parchment paper. Father is ever emotionless.

Ichabod watches them, ducking down to keep hidden . . .

Father and the Third Man walk to leave down the aisle, passing close to Ichabod without seeing him. They exit, leaving Young Ichabod alone in the silent church.

Young Ichabod rises, begins moving fearfully forward . . . **FOLLOW** as he crosses through the church . . . going to the **RED DOOR** . . . opening it . . .

115 ICHABOD'S DREAM—CHURCH, BEYOND RED DOOR—MORNING

Young Ichabod enters. The room contains **TORTURE DEVICES: IRON CUFFS, THUMB SCREWS, KNIFES** and **NEEDLES.** There is a **SPIKED CHAIR,** fitted with sharp spikes, adorned with straps for holding down the "accused."

Young Ichabod backs away, terrified, then sees . . .

A shaft of light cuts across a large, sarcophagus-like IRON MAIDEN—where MOTHER'S EYES can be seen through the slit in the Iron Maiden's face. Open eyes. Dead eyes.

Young Ichabod lets out a strangled cry, runs to the Iron Maiden, trying to pull it open, clawing at the lock . . .

Finally, Young Ichabod backs away, choking on misery. He looks around in despair. He falls to his knees at the spiked chair, places his hands on the spikes, pressing . . .

As he sobs, blood runs down from his hands. He looks down and sees the CAT is there, looking up at him. The cat reaches up to rub its head against his face.

116 INT. VAN TASSEL HOUSE, ICHABOD'S ROOM—NIGHT

Ichabod, sobbing, has jerked up out of the dream straight into Katrina's embrace.

She is sitting on the bed, holding him, calming him. She notices blood on his palms.

She takes a plain linen handkerchief from her cuff and dabs at the blood.

> KATRINA
> Hush . . . hush . . . you were dreaming.

Ichabod falls back on the pillow.

> ICHABOD
> Yes . . . things I had forgotten and would like not to remember.

> KATRINA
> Perhaps the remembering is the hard road to peace of mind . . . What ails you, Ichabod?

> ICHABOD
> I was well, it was the world that was ill . . . But since I came here . . .

> KATRINA
> You were not a happy man when you came. I think your wound was deeper than the wound you received from the Horseman . . .

(she puts her hand on his forehead)
But your fever is broken, and though I cannot cure the world I would
make you live happy in it . . . Tell me what you dreamed.

ICHABOD

How I found my mother dead . . . how good and evil sometimes wear
each other's clothes. She was an innocent, a child of nature, con-
demned . . . murdered . . . by my father . . .

KATRINA

Murdered by . . . ?

ICHABOD

Yes—murdered to save her soul! By a Bible-Black tyrant behind a mask
of righteousness. I was seven when I lost my faith.

KATRINA

What do you believe in, Ichabod?

ICHABOD

Sense and reason, cause and consequence, an ordered universe . . .
Oh lord, I should not have come to this place where my rational mind
has been so controverted by the spirit world . . .

KATRINA

Is there nothing you will take from Sleepy Hollow that was worth the
coming here?

Their eyes meet.

ICHABOD

No . . . not nothing. A kiss . . . and how rare a thing . . . a kiss from
a lovely woman before she saw my face or knew my name.

KATRINA

Yes, without sense or reason . . .

They hold still, perhaps about to kiss.

KATRINA (CONT'D)

It was a kiss on account.

But Ichabod breaks the moment.

ICHABOD

Oh—God forgive me—I talk of kisses and you have
lost your brave man Brom—

KATRINA

I have shed my tears for Brom . . . and yet my
heart is not broken. Do you think me wicked?

ICHABOD

No . . . but perhaps there is a little bit of the witch
in you, Katrina.

KATRINA

Why do you say that?

ICHABOD
Because you have bewitched me.

This time their held look turns into a passionate embrace . . .

117 EXT. VAN TASSEL HOUSE, PORCH—NIGHT

Young Masbath slowly opens the door to peer out. He walks out onto the porch, watching as . . .

ACROSS THE LAWN, a **CLOAKED FIGURE** walks, carrying a **LANTERN**. The figure heads onto the long straight road, into the forest, lantern light dissipating.

Young Masbath steps off the porch, in cautious pursuit.

118 EXT. THE HOLLOW—EARLY MORNING

Dawn light is visible over fog-shrouded forests.

119 INT. VAN TASSEL HOUSE, ICHABOD'S ROOM—MORNING

Ichabod awakes, rolls . . . finds Lady Van Tassel at his bedside with food and drink. Ichabod covers himself with his sheets.

LADY VAN TASSEL

You slept like the dead.

ICHABOD

You are too kind to me . . . I do not look to be served by the lady of
the house.

LADY VAN TASSEL

(smiles)
Nor would you be but that the servant girl has vanished.

ICHABOD

Sarah?

LADY VAN TASSEL

Run away, like many more—people are leaving in fear without ceremony.

ICHABOD

Where is . . . ?

LADY VAN TASSEL

She watched over you till dawn. Now it is her turn to sleep.

Young Masbath enters as Lady Van Tassel goes out.

Ichabod looks at his palms, which are stained with dried blood.

ICHABOD

Help me. I am fit for another day, I think.

The scene incorporates Young Masbath pouring water for Ichabod to wash
himself, and helping him into his clothes.

YOUNG MASBATH

Where are we going?

ICHABOD

To the Notary's office.

YOUNG MASBATH

Why?

ICHABOD

Because that is where I expect to find deposited . . . the last will and
testament of the elder Van Garrett . . .

YOUNG MASBATH

You have thought of something . . .

ICHABOD

. . . of something you said, Young Masbath . . . The Widow Winship
came many a day with a basket of eggs to Van Garrett . . . who
I understand had hens to spare . . . I begin to see. It was Van Garett's
child that the widow was carrying. And what news have you?

YOUNG MASBATH

I heard someone leaving last night. Looked like they headed to town,
but I lost them in the woods.

ICHABOD

You didn't see who?

YOUNG MASBATH

All I saw was their lantern.

Ichabod ponders, troubled, as Masbath brings him a shirt.

ICHABOD

The Horseman does the killing but, I believe, at the bidding of a mortal, someone of flesh and blood.

YOUNG MASBATH

What . . . ? What makes you say that?

ICHABOD

The witch . . . the crone, when I happened upon her corpse, she lay in a pool of blood. Blood poured hard from her neck. The wound was not cauterized.

YOUNG MASBATH

Then, she was not killed by the Hessian. Someone only tried to make it seem so.

ICHABOD

(nods)

It was the settling of a private score. But the Horseman cuts heads to a different drum. The crone pointed us to what drives the Hessian—his skull has been stolen from his grave. The person who stole it has power over the Hessian. Here is why the Headless One has returned through the gate of the Tree of the Dead. He chops heads until his own is restored to him.

YOUNG MASBATH

But what person . . . ?

ICHABOD

A person who stands to gain by these murders.

120 EXT. TOWN SQUARE, CHURCH—DAY

WAGONS, **HORSES** and **TOWNSPEOPLE** swarm. A **CROWD** empties the town's general store. Provisions are passed along, man to man, and loaded onto wheelbarrows.

Ichabod and Young Masbath ride, passing **MANY ANGRY FACES**.

All up and down the long straight road, home owners board up windows with lumber.

Ichabod and Young Masbath stop, tying their horses in front of the "**NOTARY**." Ichabod looks off . . .

DOWN THE ROAD, people head to the **CHURCH**. Much activity . . .

ICHABOD

Sanctuary. Or, so they hope.

People carry supplies into the church, within the bordering **WROUGHT-IRON FENCE**. Others work to build and erect massive **WOODEN CROSSES**.

In the crowd here, Reverend Steenwyck spots Ichabod and Young Masbath, pushes past people, shouting . . .

STEENWYCK

There he is! There . . . !

People begin to pay attention to Steenwyck as he climbs atop a crate, pointing toward Ichabod . . .

STEENWYCK (CONT'D)

(to everyone)
The desecrater of Christian burial!
Twice he met the Horseman, and kept his head! How is it so . . . ?

AT THE NOTARY, Ichabod tries to ignore, heads inside, as a clod of earth hits him on the shoulder.

IN THE CHURCHYARD, Steenwyck continues his rant.

STEENWYCK (CONT'D)

The Devil protects his own!

121 INT. NOTARY PUBLIC, HARDENBROOK'S OFFICES—DAY

A small, untidy room with piles of dusty documents in great disorder. The Notary Hardenbrook looks at Ichabod with his one good eye. Young Masbath stands near.

ICHABOD

I take it, Mr. Hardenbrook, that wills and testaments are held here on public record?

Hardenbrook is in a funk, trying to act calm. He passes a document across the desk.

> ### HARDENBROOK
> I believe this is what you wish to see. Take it and go!

Ichabod scans the will of Peter Van Garrett.

> ### HARDENBROOK (CONT'D)
> Van Garrett Senior left his estate to his next of kin, that is to say, to his only son. However, the son being murdered in the same instant . . .

> ### ICHABOD
> The next of kin after the son would be the eldest of the line from Van Garrett's father's sister . . . none other than Baltus Van Tassel: something else no one thought to mention!

> ### HARDENBROOK
> Well, you have found your way to it, and I hope you will leave now before my windows are broken.

The crowd murmurs outside like angry bees. Ichabod flourishes the will.

> ### ICHABOD
> I am not ready to leave.

Hardenbrook starts moaning and wringing his hands.

> ### ICHABOD (CONT'D)
> A brick through your window is not what puts you in terror, Hardenbrook . . . there is something else . . . I saw your fear, and Steenwyck's and the doctor's, when you met at Philipse's house . . . Philipse paid with his head, and you fear for your own.

> ### HARDENBROOK
> Yes, it's true!—but we did not know it was a murdering plot when we were drawn in!

> ### ICHABOD
> Drawn in by whom?!

> ### HARDENBROOK
> Mercy upon me!—We meant no harm to come to her!

> ### ICHABOD
> No harm to come to whom?

> ### HARDENBROOK
> (babbling)
> But the marriage made her next of kin . . .

> ### ICHABOD
> Made *who* next of kin to *whom*?!—I'm confused!

> ### YOUNG MASBATH
> He means old Van Garrett secretly married the Widow Winship.

ICHABOD

(getting it)

Of course! And Van Garrett made a new will, leaving everything to her and his unborn child . . . So she stood between Baltus and the legacy! Where is the will?

HARDENBROOK

I cannot be seen to help you—the Horseman will come for me—!

ICHABOD

I will not leave without the very last will and testament of—

Hardenbrook digs into a mountain of documents, hurling handfuls into the air . . . and flings the second will at Ichabod. Young Masbath nervously checks the door.

HARDENBROOK

Go, then! I am a dead man!

He starts to sob.

YOUNG MASBATH

Sir . . .

ICHABOD

(reading)

Young Masbath . . . I know now why your father died. That night when Van Garrett quarreled with his son, Jonathan Masbath was summoned upstairs to witness the new Will. Here is your father's signature. It was his death warrant.

Young Masbath takes the document and looks at it tearfully.

ICHABOD (CONT'D)

But the secret was not safe. Mrs. Killian the midwife was forewarned the baby was coming—and so she, too, had to die.

One of the other hurled documents has fluttered down fortuitously in front of Ichabod. He picks it up.

ICHABOD (CONT'D)

The marriage certificate. Parson Steenwyck married them. Doctor Lancaster confirmed the widow was pregnant. She told the secret to Magistrate Philipse. Notary Hardenbrook concealed the documents . . .

Hardenbrook snivels and moans and wrings his hands.

ICHABOD (CONT'D)

And you all kept silence! Why? . . . For some nameless dread of the man who stood to gain by it—Baltus Van Tassel!

123 INT. VAN TASSEL HOUSE, STAIRS—DAY

Ichabod and Young Masbath start up the stairs, noticing:

124 INT. VAN TASSEL HOUSE, PARLOR—DAY

Baltus, alone, with a glass of liquor, is brooding over an oak coffer of **SILVER COINS**, running coins through his fingers.

125 INT. VAN TASSEL HOUSE, STAIRS—DAY

Ichabod continues with Young Masbath, speaking quietly.

> **YOUNG MASBATH**
> I think there is some error in your reasoning . . .

> **ICHABOD**
> (politely)
> Really? Do give me the benefit of your . . .

> **YOUNG MASBATH**
> All these murders . . . just so that Baltus Van Tassel should inherit yet
> more land and property?

> **ICHABOD**
> Precisely. Men murder for profit. Possibly you don't know
> New York . . . ?

Suddenly he sees his bedroom door is ajar.

126 INT. VAN TASSEL HOUSE, ICHABOD'S BEDROOM—DAY

Ichabod's entry surprises . . . Katrina, sitting at Ichabod's desk, reading his Ledger.

> **ICHABOD**
> Katrina . . . why are you in my room?

> **KATRINA**
> (smiles)
> Because it is yours. Is it wicked of me?

> **ICHABOD**
> No . . . no . . .

> **KATRINA**
> I missed you. Where did you go?

> **ICHABOD**
> To the Notary . . . I had questions to ask Hardenbrook.

> **KATRINA**
> And did you learn anything of interest?

Ichabod and Young Masbath exchange a glance.

> **ICHABOD**
> Well . . . perhaps.

> **KATRINA**
> My father . . .

> **ICHABOD**
> (jumps)
> Your father . . . ?

> **KATRINA**
> Yes. My father thinks you should return to New York.

ICHABOD

Really? Why is that?

KATRINA

(smiles)
I don't know. Perhaps he looked in your ledger and did not like
what he saw . . .

She leaves the Ledger open on the desk. Ichabod steps over to look. Young Masbath cranes his neck
to look. It is a page of doodles with the name "Katrina" written several times, and a sketch of Katrina.
Embarrassed, Ichabod closes the Ledger.

KATRINA (CONT'D)

He believes townfolk and country do not mix.

Ichabod opens the drawer in the desk and puts away the documents he took from the Notary.

He is nervous because he knows they point to complicity by Katrina's father. Young Masbath,
watching, understands this. Ichabod locks the drawer and pockets the key.

KATRINA (CONT'D)

What have you there?

ICHABOD

Evidence. I'm sorry, I must ask your . . .

KATRINA

Then I will leave you to your thoughts. Sleep well.

Katrina leaves. Ichabod is troubled.

Then—to add to his troubles—he suddenly sees a **HUGE SPIDER** scuttling under his bed. He doesn't
like spiders, even small ones. He gives a yelp.

YOUNG MASBATH

It's only a spider.

ICHABOD

Where's it gone?—Where's it gone? Can you see it?

Young Masbath crouches to look under the bed. He frowns, puzzled.

YOUNG MASBATH

There's something under there . . .

ICHABOD

Kill it! Kill it!
(getting a grip)
No—no . . . er . . . stun it . . .

YOUNG MASBATH

Help me move the bed.

Young Masbath and Ichabod move the bed.

YOUNG MASBATH (CONT'D)

Look . . .

117

UNDER THE BED is revealed a strange **PENTAGRAM** drawn in chalk.

> YOUNG MASBATH (CONT'D)
> The Evil Eye!

> ICHABOD
> What . . . ? What is . . . ?

> YOUNG MASBATH
> It is someone casting spells against you.

> ICHABOD
> The Evil Eye . . .

The spider is sitting on the Pentagram.

127 INT. VAN TASSEL HOUSE, ICHABOD'S ROOM—LATER NIGHT

Young Masbath, fully dressed, sleeps on the bed. Ichabod sits waiting. He takes the cover off the lantern, looks at a **CLOCK**. Midnight.

Ichabod heard **A DOOR OPEN AND CLOSE**, then a **CREAK** on the stairs. He lights a candle. Then he goes to wake Young Masbath.

128 INT. VAN TASSEL HOUSE, ICHABOD'S DOOR—NIGHT

Ichabod and Young Masbath come out of the room.

129 INT. VAN TASSEL HOUSE, SECOND FLOOR HALLWAY—NIGHT

Ichabod and Young Masbath come down **STAIRS** with a lantern, cautious.

130 INT. VAN TASSEL HOUSE, SITTING ROOM—NIGHT

Ichabod and Young Masbath cross. **A CREAKING FLOORBOARD** is **HEARD** from **ANOTHER ROOM.**
Ichabod quickly covers his lantern.

Across the room, **LIGHT** comes under a **DOOR**, stops . . . continues. **FOOTSTEPS** are **HEARD,**
then a **DOOR OPENING** and **CLOSING.**

131 EXT. FOREST BY VAN TASSEL HOUSE—NIGHT

LANTERN LIGHT moves, far ahead. Ichabod and Young Masbath follow, fearful, keeping hidden.

132 EXT. FOREST BY VAN TASSEL HOUSE, FARTHER ON (HILLSIDE)—NIGHT

Ichabod and Young Masbath stop on a hillside.

> ICHABOD
>
> Wait here.

Ichabod advances, up the hill . . . peers forward to see . . .

133 EXT. FOREST CLEARING BY VAN TASSEL HOUSE—NIGHT

The lantern sits on a rock. On a blanket, a semi-naked **MAN** and semi-naked **WOMAN** are in the midst
of rough **SEX.**

Ichabod crawls to peer from underbrush.

The couple keeps coupling, the **MAN** on top. His grunts and gasps are particularly desperate.
He's all over the **WOMAN**, who lays back . . . it is **LADY VAN TASSEL.**

Ichabod swallows.

Lady Van Tassel pulls down the man's shirt, exposes his flesh. She raises a small, sharp
KNIFE behind his back.

Ichabod's eyes widen. He's about to shout a warning, but . . .

Lady Van Tassel brings the blade to her own hand, slicing deep into her palm.
Blood flows. She rubs her cut hand over her partner's arching back, smearing blood.

Lady Van Tassel caresses the man's chest, neck, face . . . trailing blood. The man lifts his
head, in ecstasy, sucking the woman's bloody fingers . . . it's **REVEREND STEENWYCK.**

Ichabod backs away, having seen more than enough.

134 EXT. FOREST BY VAN TASSEL ESTATE (HILLSIDE)—NIGHT

Ichabod returns to Young Masbath's side.

> YOUNG MASBATH
>
> What was there?

> ICHABOD
>
> Something I wish I had not seen. A beast with two backs.

> YOUNG MASBATH
>
> (wow!)
> A beast with . . . ? What next in these bewitched woods?!

135 INT. VAN TASSEL HOUSE, ICHABOD'S ROOM—NIGHT

Ichabod and Young Masbath enter.

Ichabod sees that his desk drawer is slightly open.

He opens the drawer knowing the worst.

The documents have been taken.

Masbath suddenly sniffs the air. He signals to Ichabod, alert. He sniffs again . . . and in the grate is the source of the smell: the documents burned to ashes.

Ichabod, in despondency, brings his finger to his head, rubbing his temples.

137 INT. VAN TASSEL HOUSE, KITCHEN—DAY

> **LADY VAN TASSEL**
> She will not see you.

She is talking to Ichabod. Her hand is loosely bandaged.

> **ICHABOD**
> Did she say . . . anything?

> **LADY VAN TASSEL**
> Only that she will not come down.

> **ICHABOD**
> I see. Thank you.

Ichabod turns to go.

> **LADY VAN TASSEL**
> Constable, you have not asked me how I hurt my hand since
> yesterday . . . which would have been polite. In fact you have
> been as careful not to look at it as not to mention it.

She strips off the bandage to show a roughly sewn cut.

> **ICHABOD**
> Yes—I'm sorry . . . How did you . . . ?

Lady Van Tassel **GRABS** Ichabod by the wrist, tight . . .

> **LADY VAN TASSEL**
> (whispering, close)
> I know you saw me.

> **ICHABOD**
> What . . . ?

> **LADY VAN TASSEL**
> I know you followed last night. You must promise not to tell my
> husband what you saw . . . promise me . . .

Ichabod tries to pull away, but she grips tighter. The **FRONT DOOR** is **HEARD SLAMMING**.
Ichabod is panicky.

> **LADY VAN TASSEL (CONT'D)**
> Reverend Steenwyck has power over me.

> **ICHABOD**
> P-p-power . . . ?

> **LADY VAN TASSEL**
> He knows something terrible against my dear husband—what you
> witnessed was the price of Steenwyck's silence.

> **ICHABOD**
> What does Steenwyck know?

Footsteps approach the door, the handle turns.

> **LADY VAN TASSEL**
> Later—later . . .

She pulls away just as Baltus enters.

> **BALTUS**
> The town is in a ferment. Horror piled on tragedy—Hardenbrook
> is dead—strangled.

Baltus goes straight to a flagon on the side table and lifts it to his lips. Ichabod stares at Baltus's
strong hands gripping the neck of the flagon.

> **LADY VAN TASSEL**
> Oh . . . ! That harmless old man?

> **BALTUS**
> Hanged himself in the night!

> **ICHABOD**
> Hanged himself?

> **BALTUS**
> Reverend Steenwyck has called a meeting at the church—tonight.
> Every man, woman and child.
> (to Ichabod)
> He will speak against you—if you are wise you will be gone from here.
> Steenwyck's congregation is already halfway to being a mob.

> **ICHABOD**
> I will go when I have done what I came to do.

Lady Van Tassel comes to calm her husband. Baltus notices her wound.

> **BALTUS**
> What is this?

> **LADY VAN TASSEL**
> I was careless with the kitchen knife—

> **BALTUS**
> The wound looks angry—

> **LADY VAN TASSEL**
> I'll bind it later with wild arrowroot flowers—I know where I'll find
> some. Will you ride with me?

Ichabod slips silently out of the room.

139 INT. VAN TASSEL HOUSE, STAIRS—DAY

Ichabod goes up the stairs.

139 INT. VAN TASSEL HOUSE, SECOND FLOOR—DAY

Ichabod knocks quietly at Katrina's door. No answer. He quietly opens the door.

140 INT. VAN TASSEL HOUSE, KATRINA'S ROOM—DAY

Katrina's bed has been slept in but it's empty and she is not there.

But in the grate there is the telltale heap of charred paper and ash, recognizable as Ichabod's documents.

A sound at the door makes him whip around. It is Young Masbath.

> **YOUNG MASBATH**
> I saw her riding away towards the old pasture.

141 INT. WINDMILL—DAY

A small **PILE** of **STRAW** burns. **GLOVED HANDS** unfold a paper filled with **HAIR CLIPPINGS**, which are sprinkled on the fire.

A cloaked **FIGURE** kneels at the pile. This person removes a **HUMAN SKULL** from a cloth bag.

The skull is placed at center in the flames. It's teeth are sharp, cut to points—the **HORSEMAN'S SKULL**.

142 INT. VAN TASSEL ESTATE—FIELDS—DAY

Ichabod rides Gunpowder, approaching the Ruined Cottage. He finds Katrina crouched over the hearthstone. Her horse grazes. She hears his horse and turns.

> **ICHABOD**
> Katrina . . .

Ichabod dismounts. Katrina had made a small fire. She is "doing magic." Mumbling. She turns to look at Ichabod in anger and tears.

ICHABOD (CONT'D)
(sympathetically)
You took the papers and burned them . . . ?

KATRINA
So that you would not have them to accuse my father . . . !

ICHABOD
I . . . I accuse no one . . . but if there is guilt I cannot alter it no
matter how much it grieves me . . . and no spells of yours can alter
it either . . .

KATRINA
If you knew my father you would not have such harsh thoughts about
him—no, nor if you felt anything for me!

ICHABOD
(in torment)
I am pinioned by a chain of reasoning! Why else did his four friends
conspire to conceal . . . ?

KATRINA
You are the Constable, not I—so find another chain of reasoning and
let me be.

ICHABOD

I cannot—not the one or the other. I am heartsick with it.

KATRINA

I think you have no heart—and I had a mind once to give you mine.

Katrina mounts her horse, which rears up. She is momentarily like a female warrior, her eyes ablaze with anger and tears.

ICHABOD

(cries out)

Yes—I think you loved me that day when you followed me into the Western Woods!—to have braved such peril!

KATRINA

(scornfully)

What peril was there for me if it was my own father who controlled the Headless Horseman?! Good-bye, Ichabod Crane! I curse the day you came to Sleepy Hollow!

Ichabod watches her gallop away and hides his anguished face for comfort in Gunpowder's neck.

143 EXT. FIELD AND COPSE—EVENING

A distant bell is tolling as Baltus waits on his horse . . . watching where Lady Van Tassel can be glimpsed among the spaced trees gathering "arrowroot flowers."

BALTUS

(calls out)

Come. Hurry up! The meeting bell has started tolling.

He looks anxiously toward the village, then back to the trees . . . where to his horror he sees . . . the Headless Horseman moves slowly toward Lady Van Tassel, calmly unsheathing his sword.

144 EXT. SLEEPY HOLLOW, CHURCH—NIGHT

People are entering the Church while the bell tolls them in . . . watched grimly by Steenwyck.

145 EXT. SLEEPY HOLLOW TOWN SQUARE, CHURCH—NIGHT

More people are heading toward the Church. In the shadows, Ichabod, hatted and cloaked to make himself look anonymous, also watches the people going by . . . and sees Katrina among them.

Baltus comes charging through the **TOWN SQUARE** on his horse.

BALTUS

The Horseman . . . !

Baltus is barely hanging on. He stops, falling off his horse, scrambling toward Katrina, who is not far from Ichabod . . .

> BALTUS (CONT'D)
> Save me . . .

> KATRINA
> Father . . . ?

> BALTUS
> He killed her . . .

Baltus grasps Katrina, deathly afraid.

> BALTUS (CONT'D)
> The Horseman has killed your stepmother!

HOOFBEATS are HEARD . . . the SCREECHY CRY of Daredevil. Baltus looks . . .

The Horseman rides into view, giving chase . . .

Instant mayhem—the few people in the churchyard flee, heading for the Church . . .

Baltus runs toward the Church . . .

> KATRINA
> Father!

Katrina chases after Baltus. Ichabod now sees that his "case" is falling apart. He and Young Masbath start running to the Church.

146 INT. CHURCH—NIGHT

The GATHERERS in the pews react to the commotion, shouting, some running to the windows . . . to the doors . . .

147 EXT. CHURCH—NIGHT

Baltus pushes through the IRON GATE, across the churchyard, bounding up the stairs . . . Katrina following him.

The Horseman rides behind . . .

Ichabod, with Masbath, follow into the churchyard. Ichabod glances back . . .

> ICHABOD
> (to Young Masbath)
> I know what you are thinking.

> YOUNG MASBATH
> It seems Baltus Van Tassel is not the one who controls the Horseman.

As the Horseman reaches the open gate, Daredevil rears up violently, snorting, unwilling to enter.

148 INT. CHURCH—NIGHT

Baltus makes his way into the church, shoving people aside.

Men pass **RIFLES** from stockpiles and climb onto pews at the boarded windows. Women herd children into a cellar.

Baltus searches for a hiding place, moves toward the back . . .

Katrina moves through, following Baltus . . .

At the front of the Church, Ichabod squeezes in just as the front doors are forced shut. Ichabod surveys the madness . . .

Ichabod runs to a window, looking out between boards . . .

149 EXT. CHURCH—NIGHT

At the churchyard gates, the Horseman grabs Daredevil's reins, tries to move forward again. Same result—Daredevil freaks.

The Horseman gives his **AXE** an underhand toss . . . to the ground inside the gate . . .

The axe instantly **BEGINS TO DEGRADE**—like dust in the rain.

The Horseman steers away, keeping outside the fence.

150 INT. CHURCH—NIGHT

Ichabod comes away from the window, looking to the mass of panicked citizens. He sees Katrina pushing up the aisle . . . she's heading toward Baltus.

Katrina turns to Ichabod, her face aflame with accusation.

Ichabod is humbled, desperate to make it up—but Katrina runs toward . . . the Altar, where she prostrates herself, evidently in a paroxysm of despair.

RIFLES BOOM LOUDLY as men at the windows begin **FIRING** . . .

151 EXT. CHURCH—NIGHT

The Horseman circles, under fire.

Great clouds of gun smoke shoot from the Church.

Men fire down from the belfry.

Parts of the Horseman and Daredevil splatter red as slugs hit, without effect.

At the other side of the Church . . .

The Horseman circles, heading to the town square . . .

152 INT. CHURCH—NIGHT

Riflemen shout to each other, running to the opposite windows to follow the Horseman.

Young Masbath grabs a rifle, leaps to join the brigade.

Baltus is trying to force his way to one of the cellar doors, when Steenwyck grips him angrily, **SHOVES** him . . .

> STEENWYCK
> You'll kill us all . . . !

Baltus stumbles back, topples pews.

> STEENWYCK (CONT'D)
> You're the one the Horseman wants.

Steenwyck grabs Baltus, dragging him to the front.

Ichabod's pushing past people, trying to get to them.

153 EXT. TOWN SQUARE, CHURCH—NIGHT

The Horseman brings Daredevil to a halt, yanks a large coil of **ROPE** off a hitching post, turns to ride back . . .

154 INT. CHURCH—NIGHT

Baltus pulls free from Steenwyck, falls to the floor again.

> STEENWYCK
> Why should we die for you? Get out!

Others join the rage, pulling Baltus toward the front of the Church, shouting. Ichabod joins in, struggling to push people off of Baltus . . .

ICHABOD

Stop this . . . !

Ichabod gets to Baltus's side, trying to protect.

ICHABOD (CONT'D)

The Horseman cannot enter! It does not matter who he wants,
he cannot cross the gate . . . !

At the windows, **ONE RIFLEMAN** cries out.

ONE RIFLEMAN

He's coming back!

More panic. Steenwyck points toward Baltus.

STEENWYCK

We have to save ourselves . . . !

Baltus pulls the **PISTOL** from Ichabod's holster . . .

BALTUS

No! Unhand me! Stand off . . . !

Baltus brandishes the gun. Everyone backs off.

155 EXT. CHURCH—NIGHT

The Horseman rides past the front, fired upon . . .

The Horseman halts along a length of the wrought gate, reaches . . . yanks off one **IRON POST**,
which is pointed on top, like an arrow head.

156 INT. CHURCH—NIGHT

Baltus holds everyone away with the pistol, enraged . . .

BALTUS

The next person to lay hands on me will have a bullet.

Doctor Lancaster, who so far has just been one of the crowd, now pushes his way between Steenwyck
and Baltus.

DOCTOR LANCASTER

Enough have died already!
(to Steenwyck meaningfully)
It is time to confess our sins and ask God to forgive our trespasses!

STEENWYCK

Don't be a fool! I warn you, Doctor Lancaster—!

BALTUS

(to Doctor Lancaster)
What is it that you know?

DOCTOR LANCASTER

(to Baltus)
Your four friends played you false. We were devilishly possessed by
one who—

That's as far as he gets before Steenwyck wrenches a heavy ornate **CROSS** from the wall and smashes his skull with a blow of tremendous force, with the Cross.

Baltus **FIRES**—blasts a bloody hole in Steenwyck's stomach . . . !

Everyone backs farther away as Steenwyck falls. Steenwyck lays gasping, eyes huge. He tries to crawl . . .

Katrina rises to her feet and stands, staring wide-eyed at the horror. Ichabod moves toward her.

Steenwyck lays still with a bloody gurgle, face down. Baltus looks to all the horrified people around him.

> **BALTUS**
> There is conspiracy here! And I will seek it out!

CRASH!—the **IRON POST** comes **SPEARING** through a window, trailing rope . . .

CRACK—SKEWERS Baltus from behind: its bloodied point bursting out through his breast bone . . .

Baltus gasps, stunned . . . he drops the gun, looks down to clutch the post. Blood streams out of his mouth.

Ichabod catches Katrina as she swoons. Horrorstruck, he hugs her . . . and thus notices that hanging on a ribbon around her neck is the little carved bauble taken from the neck of the dead Crone. Almost at the same time, Ichabod sees that on the flagstones where Katrina was lying there is now a "Drawing" done in chalk, identical to the "Evil Eye" drawing he found under his bed.

> **ICHABOD**
> (gasps)
> The Evil Eye again!

At that moment, a piece of White Chalk falls from Katrina's senseless hand.

> **ICHABOD (CONT'D)**
> Oh God . . . it was you!

The full horrible implication of this hits Ichabod just as:

The rope tied to the post suddenly **YANKS** Baltus backward with incredible force—**SLAMS** him into the **WINDOW** . . .

157 EXT. CHURCH—NIGHT

Baltus **CRASHES** backward through the window, hits the ground, **DRAGGED** . . .

OUTSIDE THE FENCE, the Horseman rides Daredevil away from the church, with the rope tied around Daredevil's saddle pommel . . .

Baltus **SLAMS** the fence. The rope **SNAPS**. Baltus is held there awkwardly, gurgling blood.

158 INT. CHURCH—NIGHT

Ichabod, holding Katrina, cries out—

> ICHABOD
>
> Oh . . . Katrina . . . Oh God, forgive her . . .

159 EXT. CHURCH—NIGHT

The Horseman turns Daredevil, riding back . . . his sword raised high . . .

. . . he chops off Baltus's head.

160 INT. VAN TASSEL HOUSE—NIGHT

Katrina lies insensible in her bed . . . the ribbon with the bauble around her neck.

Ichabod stands watching her, alone with his grief and his appalling "secret."

> ICHABOD
>
> It was an evil spirit possessed you. I pray God it is satisfied now, and
> that you find peace. Good-bye, Katrina. The Evil Eye has done its
> work. My life is over—spared for a lifetime of horrors in my sleep,
> waking each day to grief.

Ichabod leaves the room, closing the door.

162 EXT. VAN TASSEL HOUSE, KITCHEN, PORCH AND LAWN—DAWN

Ichabod, watched only by Young Masbath, stands by a **FIRE** burning in a **CIRCLE** of **ROCKS** nearby.
He has his Ledger. After a moment, he throws the **LEDGER** onto the fire. The pages catch quickly.

He opens his satchel and digs out a **BOOK**. His luggage is packed on the porch.

He walks back to the fire, looks at the book in his hand, the book Katrina gave him. He stands staring down.

A **DECREPIT COACH** is arriving.

163 EXT. VAN TASSEL HOUSE, KITCHEN, PORCH AND LAWN—DAY

The decrepit **COACH**, with Gunpowder as one of its team, waits, loaded with Ichabod's baggage.

Van Ripper, the driver, helps Ichabod with strapping the load. Young Masbath watches, not helping.

Ichabod turns to Young Masbath.

Angry tears come to Young Masbath's eyes. The farewell is like an argument.

> YOUNG MASBATH
>
> But who will look for the truth when you have gone?

> ICHABOD
>
> There is no more truth to be found. That is why I can go and leave
> this wretched place behind me.

> YOUNG MASBATH
>
> You think it was Katrina, don't you?

Ichabod clamps his hand over Young Masbath's mouth. He looks intently into his eyes.

> ICHABOD
>
> That can never be uttered. Never.

Ichabod takes his hand away.

> **YOUNG MASBATH**
>
> A strange sort of witch!—with a kind and loving heart! How can you think so?

> **ICHABOD**
>
> I have a good reason.

> **YOUNG MASBATH**
>
> Then you are bewitched by reason!

> **ICHABOD**
>
> I am beaten down by it! It's a hard lesson for a hard world, and you had better learn it, Young Masbath—villainy wears many masks, none so dangerous as the mask of virtue. Farewell!

Van Ripper climbs onto the coach. Ichabod looks to the Manor House. Only one light shines, in a **SECOND FLOOR WINDOW.**

Ichabod climbs into the coach.

164 INT. VAN RIPPER'S COACH—DAY

INSIDE THE COACH, Ichabod slumps. He pounds twice on the coach wall.

165 EXT. VAN TASSEL HOUSE, FRONT LAWN—DAY

OUTSIDE, Van Ripper whips the reins. The coach starts. Young Masbath watches, wiping tears.

166 INT. VAN TASSEL HOUSE, KATRINA'S ROOM—DAY

Katrina wakes. She hears the Coach Wheels. She gets up from the bed and goes to the window. Her **POV** shows the Coach leaving . . . Katrina's face shows that her world has collapsed around her.

167 EXT. TOWN SQUARE, CHURCH—DAY

Van Ripper's coach crosses the covered bridge . . . past the town square . . . past the church.

Near Doctor Lancaster's house, the coach passes a flat cart . . . on which lies the headless corpse of Lady Van Tassel. Ichabod looks at the corpse and he notes the gashed palm of one dead hand.

The cart is being pulled at a walking pace by a single horse. The **CART MAN** walking, holding the bridle.

The cart man pauses, seeing a **RIDER** approaching, traveling in the same direction as Ichabod's coach.

Ichabod realizes that the rider is Katrina. He looks from the coach window and sees Katrina get down from the horse and go to the cart.

Ichabod pulls back from his window and closes his eyes.

168 INT. VAN TASSEL HOUSE, ICHABOD'S ROOM—DAY

Young Masbath enters, looks around the empty room. He goes to sit, crosses his arms on the desk and lays down his head.

169 INT. VAN TASSEL HOUSE, PARLOR—DAY

Katrina enters. She crosses, slumps in a chair, staring into the burning fireplace.

170 INT. VAN TASSEL HOUSE, VARIOUS ROOMS—POV—DAY

A POV MOVES SLOWLY THROUGH THE HOUSE; SOMEONE'S searching various rooms . . .

171 INT. VAN RIPPER'S COACH—DAY

Ichabod opens his satchel, takes out a bottle of water and gulps from it. In replacing the bottle, he finds . . . the Book given him by Katrina. He opens the book. There is a **DIAGRAM DRAWING** on a whole page. Ichabod recognizes . . . the "Drawing" of the supposed "Evil Eye," identical to the two we have seen before. But what gets Ichabod's real attention is the bold "headline."

The Headline over the Picture is "For The Protection of A Loved One Against Evil Spirits."

Ichabod gasps, and mutters the words aloud.

What a fool he's been!

> **ICHABOD**
> (to himself)
> But then, who . . . ?

He is puzzled. He stares at his open palms. The scars on his palms trigger a thought . . .

Then he understands: something we will soon understand.

He slides the front window panel to shout through it.

> **ICHABOD (CONT'D)**
> Van Ripper, turn the coach . . . !

> **VAN RIPPER**
> What?

> **ICHABOD**
> Turn around, now!

172 INT. VAN TASSEL HOUSE, VARIOUS ROOMS, PARLOR—POV—EVENING

SOMEONE still moves through the house, a **TRAVELING POV**—moving through **ROOMS** on the ground floor . . .

Stopping at the doorway of the **PARLOR**, looking to where Katrina is seated across the room.

173 INT. DOCTOR'S RESIDENCE, MEDICAL ROOM—EVENING

Mrs. Lancaster comes to answer **BANGING** on the door. She opens the door and Ichabod pushes past, satchel in hand, taking Mrs. Lancaster's lantern.

> **ICHABOD**
> Pardon my intrusion . . .

There are **TWO COFFINS** on the floor.

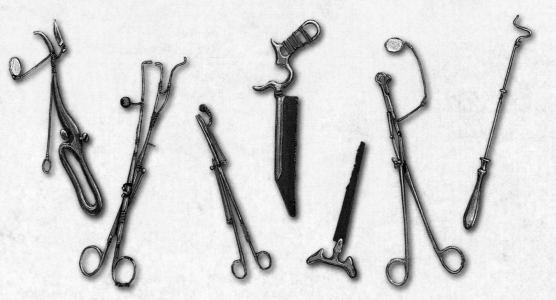

Ichabod throws off the lids from the coffins, looking to the headless **BODIES** of **BALTUS** and **LADY VAN TASSEL**.

174 INT. VAN TASSEL HOUSE, PARLOR—INTERCUT—EVENING

Katrina still sits, her eyes closed. A **FIGURE** in **BLACK** moves forward in the darkness behind . . .

175 INT. DOCTOR'S RESIDENCE, MEDICAL ROOM—INTERCUT—EVENING

Ichabod goes to lift Lady Van Tassel's hand with the **GASH** on its palm, bends to study . . . pulling at the sewn wound—pulling the stitches apart between his thumbs . . .

Mrs. Lancaster watches.

176 INT. VAN TASSEL HOUSE, PARLOR—INTERCUT—EVENING

Katrina hears a **BOARD CREAK**. She sits up, turning . . .

> KATRINA
> Who is it?

177 INT. DOCTOR'S RESIDENCE, MEDICAL ROOM—INTERCUT—EVENING

Ichabod releases the corpse's hand, tears off his spectacles, shaken by the realization . . .

> ICHABOD
> No bloodflow, no clotting, no healing . . . When this cut was
> made . . . this woman was already dead.

Ichabod grabs his satchel, bolts out the door . . .

178 INT. VAN TASSEL HOUSE, PARLOR—INTERCUT—EVENING

The **FIGURE** moves closer in darkness . . .

> KATRINA
> Who is there . . . ?

The **FIGURE** comes into the dim, flickering fire light . . . Lady Van Tassel.

> LADY VAN TASSEL
> Dear stepdaughter . . .

Katrina stands, terrified, trying to form words . . . Lady Van Tassel cackles like a witch.

> LADY VAN TASSEL (CONT'D)
> You look as if you've seen a ghost.

Katrina's eyes roll up as she **FAINTS** dead away to the floor.

179 EXT. TOWN SQUARE, DOCTOR'S RESIDENCE—EVENING

Ichabod runs out from the **DOCTOR'S RESIDENCE**, leaps up onto the empty coach, pushing Van Ripper's rifle aside. Van Ripper's urinating against the side of the building.

> VAN RIPPER
> Be with you in a minute, Constable.

Ichabod whips the horses, driving the coach away.

Van Ripper frowns in confusion.

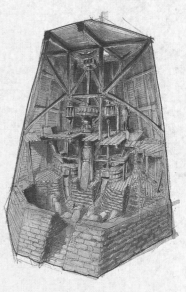

180 INT. THE WINDMILL—NIGHT

The interior of the windmill is large and shadowy, with lots of old junk, clutter, machinery, boxes, etc.

Katrina lies unconscious. Lady Van Tassel comes to cut off a clump of Katrina's hair with **SCISSORS**, grinning as she does it.

A **CONJURING PILE** has been prepared, containing a small **ANIMAL'S HEART** with an iron **NAIL** through it. Lady Van Tassel adds Katrina's hair, lights the pile off a lantern.

Lady Van Tassel **WHISPERS** over the fire. She looks to Katrina, who stirs.

Lady Van Tassel takes the **HORSEMAN'S SKULL** from a bag over her shoulder, places it in the flames. **THUNDER** is **HEARD**.

> **LADY VAN TASSEL**
> (whispers and chants)
> Rise up once more, my Dark Avenger!—Rise up!—One more night of Beheading!—Rise up with your sword, and your Mistress of the Night will make you whole—a head for a head, my unholy Horseman—rise—rise—rise from the earth, come forth again through the Tree of the Dead . . . come now for . . . Katrina!

181 EXT. WESTERN WOODS, TREE OF THE DEAD—NIGHT

The **WIND** scatters dead leaves. The **TWISTED TREE OPENS WIDE** with a **RUMBLE—SHAFTS** of **LIGHT** shooting out.

182 EXT. THE ROAD TO VAN TASSEL ESTATE—NIGHT

Ichabod drives the coach hard ahead.

183 INT. THE WINDMILL—NIGHT

Katrina sits up, groggy, looking around . . . sees the dying fire, and Lady Van Tassel watching her.

> **LADY VAN TASSEL**
> Awake at last. Did you think it was all a nasty dream? Alas, no.

> **KATRINA**
> My father saw the Horseman kill you . . .

> **LADY VAN TASSEL**
> He saw the Horseman coming to me with his sword unsheathed. But it is I who govern the Horseman, my dear, and Baltus did not stay to see.

> **KATRINA**
> But there was your body!

> **LADY VAN TASSEL**
> The servant girl, Sarah. I always thought her useless, but she turned out useful. Tomorrow I'll totter out of the woods and spin a tale how I found Baltus and Sarah in the act of lust . . . as I watched, the Horseman was upon them, and off went Sarah's head! I fainted and remember nothing more . . .

139

Sleepy Hollow Town Elders

1. Baltus Van Tassel
   wealth, land, influence

2. Samuel Philipse
   town magistrate

3. Dr. Thomas Lancaster
   medical doctor

4. Reverend Steenwyck
   clergyman

5. James Hardenbrook
   notary public

Evidence
handled properly

> KATRINA
>
> *Who are you?*

> LADY VAN TASSEL
>
> My family name was . . . Archer.

> KATRINA
>
> (remembering the cottage hearth)
> The Archer . . .

> LADY VAN TASSEL
>
> I lived with my father and mother and my sister in a gamekeeper's
> cottage not far from here . . .

The conversation is being heard by a **MOVING POV** among the shadows.

> LADY VAN TASSEL (CONT'D)
>
> Until one day, my father died, and the landlord who received many
> years of loyal service from my parents . . . evicted us. No one in this
> God-fearing town would take us in . . .

The **MOVING POV** stops, spying from behind the clutter. The **REVERSE SHOT** reveals
YOUNG MASBATH, holding his breath.

> LADY VAN TASSEL (CONT'D)
>
> . . . because my mother was suspected of witchcraft . . .

Young Masbath looks about for a weapon. His eyes alight on a large Wooden Mallet.

> LADY VAN TASSEL (CONT'D)
>
> She was no witch, but I believe she knew much that lies under the
> surface of life . . . and she schooled her daughters well while we lived
> as outcasts in the Western Woods. She died within a year . . . and my
> sister and I remained in our refuge, seeing not a soul . . . until,
> gathering firewood one day, we crossed the path of the Hessian . . .

184 FLASHBACK—FOREST BATTLEFIELD (WESTERN WOODS)—DAY

The Hessian Horseman (avec head) has happened upon **TWO YOUNG GIRLS** gathering firewood.
The girls stand frozen at the sight of him, till one girl drops her firewood and runs . . .

The second girl remains, holding the Horseman's gaze.

185 INT. WINDMILL—NIGHT

> LADY VAN TASSEL
>
> I saw his death, and from that moment . . .

186 FLASHBACK—FOREST BATTLEFIELD (WESTERN WOODS)—DAY

The Girl watches the burial of the Horseman . . . and his Head dropped into the grave.

> LADY VAN TASSEL
>
> . . . I offered my soul to Satan if he would raise the Hessian from the grave to avenge me.

187 INT. WINDMILL—NIGHT

Young Masbath, unseen, works his way quietly around behind Lady Van Tassel.

> **KATRINA**
>
> Avenge you?

> **LADY VAN TASSEL**
>
> Against Van Garrett, who evicted my family, against Baltus Van Tassel who, with wife and simpering girlchild, stole our home. I swore I would make myself mistress of all they had . . .
> (she cackles again)
> The easiest part was the first—to enter your house as your mother's sick nurse and put her body into the grave, and my own into the marriage bed.

Katrina cries out in horror.

> **LADY VAN TASSEL (CONT'D)**
>
> Not quite so easy was to secure my legacy . . . but lust delivered Reverend Steenwyck into my power. Fear did the same for the Notary Hardenbrook. The drunken Philipse succumbed for a share of the proceeds, and the Doctor's silence I exchanged for my complicity in his fornications . . .

Masbath moves into the open, weapon raised. Katrina sees him and stifles a gasp.

> **KATRINA**
>
> (keeping Lady Van Tassel's attention)
> Yes!—you have everything now.

> **LADY VAN TASSEL**
>
> No, my dear—you do, by your father's will. But I get everything in the event of your death!
> (she cackles again)

Lady Van Tassel's hand reaches for the Mystic Bauble on Katrina's neck. She rips it free.

> **LADY VAN TASSEL (CONT'D)**
>
> (as she does so)
> This pretty bauble, which I so kindly gave you to wear, has done it's work. My sister, by the way, sadly passed away . . .

188 FLASHBACK—OUTSIDE CRONE'S CAVE HOME—DAY

The Crone falls to the ground outside her cave, unconscious, beaten and bloodied.

A hand—Lady Van Tassel's hand—enters **FRAME** to haul the Crone up by the hair, and **WE SEE** the Crone's bloodied features face to face with the wicked smile of Lady Van Tassel.

189 INT. WINDMILL—NIGHT

> **LADY VAN TASSEL**
>
> . . . quite recently.

190 FLASHBACK—OUTSIDE CRONE'S CAVE HOME—DAY

Lady Van Tassel holds a **SWORD** high, **SWINGS DOWN** . . . Then we see the separated Head and Torso . . . and the severed **CORD**, which had been around the Crone's neck . . . and Lady Van Tassel's Hand reaching for the Mystic Bauble, which had fallen free.

191 INT. WINDMILL—NIGHT

Young Masbath is about ready to bring the mallet down upon Lady Van Tassel's head.

> **KATRINA**
> (keeping Lady Van Tassel's attention)
> It was the Crone you killed . . . your own sister . . .

> **LADY VAN TASSEL**
> She brought it upon herself . . .

Like a whiplash, Lady Van Tassel turns cackling at Young Masbath—she sensed him by witchery!

> **LADY VAN TASSEL (CONT'D)**
> (to Young Masbath)
> —by helping you and your master!

Young Masbath shrieks and drops the mallet.

> **LADY VAN TASSEL (CONT'D)**
> You are just in time to have your head sliced off!

Katrina and Young Masbath run to each other for mutual comfort.

LIGHTNING BRIGHTENS the forest. Lady Van Tassel looks up.

> **LADY VAN TASSEL (CONT'D)**
> The Horseman comes. And tonight he comes for you!

192 EXT. WESTERN WOODS—NIGHT

The Horseman rides Daredevil, a freight train of moldering flesh . . .

193 INT. WINDMILL—NIGHT

Katrina and Young Masbath are holding hands, scared.

Lady Van Tassel picks up the Horseman's skull in her gloved hand and puts up her face and gives out a long animal howl. Distantly, Daredevil is heard answering with a scream.

Katrina and Young Masbath run. Lady Van Tassel has no need to stop them.

> **LADY VAN TASSEL**
> Run! There is no escape!

194 EXT. VAN TASSEL HOUSE, PORCH AND LAWN—NIGHT

Ichabod leaps from the coach, bounds up porch stairs . . .

> **ICHABOD**
> Katrina!

Ichabod stops, sees **FIRELIGHT** at the Windmill. He runs . . . leaps back up to the coach and takes off . . .

195 EXT. WINDMILL—NIGHT

THUNDER BOOMS. WIND HOWLS. Lady Van Tassel stands in the doorway with the skull in one hand, laughing.

196 EXT. AROUND THE OTHER SIDE OF THE WINDMILL—NIGHT

Katrina and Young Masbath break out into the open. Ichabod drives toward them . . .

> **KATRINA**
> Ichabod!

Ichabod meets them, halts the coach and jumps down (as the coach horses trot away), running to put his arms around Katrina and Young Masbath . . .

> **ICHABOD**
> Thank God . . .

Lady Van Tassel's mad laughter is heard. Ichabod and Katrina turn as . . .

Lady Van Tassel rides from around the windmill on her white horse. She shrieks with laughter.

ALONG THE TREELINE, the Horseman breaks into the open . . . Hell on horseback—full speed ahead . . .

> **LADY VAN TASSEL (O.S.)**
> Have you come back to arrest him after all?!

Ichabod thinks fast, moving to the windmill, leading Katrina and Young Masbath along with him.

ICHABOD

Quickly . . . !

Behind, wind tosses Lady Van Tassel's dress and hair. She holds the Horseman's skull high.

LADY VAN TASSEL

Mind your hat, Constable!

Young Masbath scurries up the ladder and in.

Katrina's next. Ichabod looks behind . . . The Horseman is almost upon them.

Ichabod follows Katrina, pulling himself up. The Horseman arrives, dismounting, moving forward . . .

197 INT. WINDMILL—NIGHT

Ichabod leaps up, lifts the heavy trap door on its hinges, slams it. The door is **POUNDED** from outside, buckling.

YOUNG MASBATH

It won't hold.

Ichabod goes to a large **GRINDSTONE** against a wall. He struggles to roll it . . .

Young Masbath helps him roll it to the trap door. It falls on top with a **THUD**. Masbath jumps back as the Horseman's sword jabs up through the grindstone's center hole.

The sword withdraws. **POUNDING** begins anew.

198 INT. WINDMILL—NIGHT

The Horseman chops at the door with his axe.

199 INT. WINDMILL—NIGHT

POUNDING CONTINUES, Katrina and Young Masbath back away. Ichabod holds his lantern up, desperate for ideas, searching.

Above, to the right, is the high **MILLING PLATFORM**, where grain is ground and bagged, and a ladder leading to it. To the left is the crooked, open **STAIRCASE**.

Ichabod picks up a **BAILING HOOK**, a plan forming. He gives his lantern to Katrina and points.

> **ICHABOD**
> Get up those stairs. Open the door to the roof and wait.

Katrina and Young Masbath obey, heading left. Ichabod crosses to the right, starts climbing the ladder to the milling platform . . .

On the platform, Ichabod grasps a wooden lever, pulling it.

The entire windmill **CREAKS** and **GROANS** as massive **GEARS** and **COUNTERWHEELS** above begin to turn.

200 EXT. WINDMILL—NIGHT

The windmill's rotors slowly begin spinning.

UNDER THE WINDMILL, the Horseman keeps chopping . . .

His axe exposes grindstone, throwing sparks.

201 INT. WINDMILL—NIGHT

Katrina looks down from the stairway. The **POUNDING** on the trap door causes the grindstone to jump.

> KATRINA
> Ichabod . . .

> ICHABOD
> Keep climbing. I will follow . . .
>   (under his breath)
> Hopefully.

Ichabod drags large **BAGS** of **GRAIN**, lining them up at the edge of the milling platform.

ABOVE, Young Masbath throws open the door to the roof.

BELOW, Ichabod uses the bailing hook to cut holes into the grain bags, so that **MILLED GRAIN SPILLS** out and falls to the floor, creating clouds of grain dust . . .

Ichabod grabs one open bag, dumps it.

He slices into a sack hanging from a pulley system, pushes it so it swings in circles, grain flooding out . . .

More and more **DUST RISES**, filling the air . . .

202 EXT. WINDMILL ROOF—NIGHT

Masbath and Katrina come out. Rotors spin behind them.

203 INT. WINDMILL—NIGHT

The **GRINDSTONE** blocking the trap door **FALLS THROUGH** as wood splinters and gives. A moment, then the Horseman climbs in.

> **KATRINA**
> (looking in from above)
> Behind you!

Ichabod looks down, sees the Horseman, then looks to the staircase adjacent from the high platform.
He runs . . .

He **LEAPS** across the space between the platform and stairs . . .

Ichabod grasps the outer rail of the staircase, hanging on, pulls himself up onto the stairs . . .

Below, the Horseman moves through clouds of billowing dust, runs and **LEAPS**, incredibly high . . .

The Horseman grasps a hanging chain, swinging, his momentum carrying him in a wide arc . . .

Above, Ichabod runs upstairs, to the roof door.

The Horseman's weight swings him toward the stairwell . . .

He releases the chain . . . airborne momentarily . . .

The Horseman lands high up on the stairwell.

204 EXT. WINDMILL ROOF—NIGHT

Katrina and Young Masbath help Ichabod onto the roof.

> **KATRINA**
> Quickly, close it.

> **ICHABOD**
> No . . .

Ichabod takes the lantern from Katrina.

> **ICHABOD (CONT'D)**
> (points)
> Get to the crest of the roof and be ready to jump.

> **YOUNG MASBATH**
> Jump? From up here?!

205 INT. WINDMILL—NIGHT

The Horseman clomps upstairs, axe in hand.

206 EXT. WINDMILL ROOF—NIGHT

Ichabod shepherds Katrina and Young Masbath to the edge, where the rotors spin close.

> **ICHABOD**
> Jump for the sails! Wait till I give the word!

> **KATRINA**
> Ichabod! . . . I can't . . .

> **ICHABOD**
> Yes, you can, my love—hand in hand . . .

Ichabod moves back to the trap door.

Katrina and Young Masbath look at the rotors, and down at the long distance between them and the ground.

> ICHABOD (CONT'D)
> Be ready . . .

Ichabod **DROPS** the **LANTERN** into the windmill and runs . . .

> ICHABOD (CONT'D)
> Now!

207 INT. WINDMILL—NIGHT

The Horseman continues up. The lantern falls past . . .

208 EXT. WINDMILL, ROOF—NIGHT

Young Masbath jumps. Ichabod grips Katrina, jumps . . .

They hit one rotor, gripping the frame and cloth as the rotor begins its **DOWNWARD TURN** . . .

209 INT. WINDMILL—NIGHT

The lantern hits the ground and shatters—**FLAMES EXPLODE**!

Throughout the windmill's interior, grain dust is consumed instantaneously—**FLAMES ROAR** upward . . .

FLAMES engulf the Horseman . . .

210 EXT. WINDMILL—NIGHT

The rotor is halfway to its lowest point. Masbath, Katrina and Ichabod hang on as the **ENTIRE STRUCTURE TREMBLES** . . .

Flames shoot out windows, doors and seams!

On the rotor, Ichabod struggles to keep a grip on Katrina. Masbath drops. Ichabod and Katrina fall . . .

They all hit the ground. Ichabod rolls over, gasping, holding his shoulder, getting to his feet . . .

Ichabod, Katrina and Young Masbath run away as smoldering debris rains down.

211 EXT. ACROSS THE FIELD—NIGHT

Ichabod ushers them along as they run, heading uphill. Lightning flashes across the sky. **THUNDER RUMBLES.**

212 EXT. WINDMILL—NIGHT

Behind, the **WINDMILL** begins to **CRUMBLE**, huge burning sections crashing to the ground.

213 EXT. ACROSS THE FIELD—NIGHT

Ichabod, Katrina and Young Masbath slow, looking back at the incredible conflagration.

> **YOUNG MASBATH**
> Is he dead?

> **ICHABOD**
> He was dead to start with—that's the problem.

> **KATRINA**
> Look . . . !

214 EXT. WINDMILL—NIGHT

IN THE WINDMILL RUBBLE, the Horseman **RISES**, shoving off burning debris. His flame-ravaged uniform smolders.

215 EXT. ACROSS THE FIELD—NIGHT

Ichabod spins, searching for possibilities . . . He spots the **COACH** and **HORSES** not too far away . . .

> **ICHABOD**
> Come on!

They flee toward the coach. Behind . . .

Daredevil rides to rejoin the Horseman.

216 EXT. THE ROAD FROM VAN TASSEL ESTATE—NIGHT

The coach hits the long straight road, rumbling at top speed away from the Van Tassel Estate, into the forest . . .

Katrina and Masbath hold on as the coach shakes violently.

> **KATRINA**
> Where are we going?

> **ICHABOD**
> Anywhere!

> **YOUNG MASBATH**
> He's right behind!

Behind on the trail, the Horseman chases, closing fast.

> **KATRINA**
> Make for the church!

> **ICHABOD**
> We'll never reach it!

Young Masbath grabs Ichabod's satchel, offers it . . .

> **YOUNG MASBATH**
> Here, sir . . . you must have something in your
> bag of tricks.

> **ICHABOD**
> Nothing that will help us, I am afraid. Take
> the reins . . .

Young Masbath takes them. Ichabod gives Van Ripper's rifle to Katrina, then crawls back across the coach roof.

Ichabod gets to a baggage area at the rear, struggling to open a storage box.

Behind, the Horseman draws his sword, closer.

Ichabod opens the box and pulls out a jagged **HAND SAW**.

> **KATRINA**
> Look out . . . !

Ichabod looks. The Horseman rides up, **SWINGS** his sword . . .

Ichabod recoils—**THWACK**—just missed.

The Horseman lets the coach get ahead, shifting to the other side of the trail . . . coming along side again . . .

Ichabod backpedals, looking to Masbath.

> **ICHABOD**
> Keep him off! Block him!

Masbath guides the horses over. The Horseman must fall behind to avoid the wheels.

One wheel hits a large rock . . .

Ichabod bounces, falling, drops the saw . . .

He hangs off the side of the coach.

The saw clatters away on the trail.

Ichabod tries for better purchase. He grips the coach door.

Katrina climbs to offer her hand.

> **KATRINA**
> Take my hand!

Ichabod reaches to her, but the coach door falls open . . .

Ichabod's **PISTOL** falls from the holster and is lost on the trail.

Ichabod clings helplessly to the door as branches slam him.

217 EXT. BEHIND THE TRAIL

The Horseman gets to his feet. Ahead, Daredevil stands waiting, giving a **SCREECH**.

218 EXT. AHEAD ON THE TRAIL NEAR THE TREE OF THE DEAD

Katrina and Ichabod rejoin Masbath, climb off the coach to examine the ruined wheel, panicked.

> **ICHABOD**
> This is not good.

> **YOUNG MASBATH**
> We're doomed.

> **ICHABOD**
> We have to get out of the open somehow.
> Quick, follow me . . .

They turn to run, but suddenly falter, seeing . . . Riding over the crest of the hill, comes Lady Van Tassel, on her white horse, with Ichabod's lost pistol in her hand . . .

219 EXT. NEAR FOREST—NIGHT

> **LADY VAN TASSEL**
> What? Still alive?!

Across the distance, the Horseman strides in this direction.

> **ICHABOD**
> Run, Katrina . . .

Lady Van Tassel points her gun at Katrina.

> **LADY VAN TASSEL**
> Yes, do run. And jump. And skip.
> (she takes aim)
> And now let's see a somersault!

> **ICHABOD**
> Run!

Ichabod makes a move toward Lady Van Tassel, but Lady Van Tassel aims and **FIRES**—shoots Ichabod in the chest! Ichabod goes down . . .

> **KATRINA**
> No!

Young Masbath cries out, falls to his knees beside Ichabod. Katrina moves toward Ichabod . . . Lady Van Tassel rides forward—**GRABS** Katrina by the hair, **PULLING HER**, riding off toward the Horseman . . . Ichabod lays clutching the smoldering wound in his chest, gasping. Young Masbath holds him . . .

> **YOUNG MASBATH**
> Oh, God . . . no . . . no . . .

Lady Van Tassel drags Katrina by the hair as Katrina screams and struggles and kicks.

The Horseman keeps coming . . .

Lady Van Tassel stops her horse, halfway to the Horseman, drops Katrina and starts riding back, shouting . . .

> **LADY VAN TASSEL**
> There she is. Take her, she's yours!

Katrina gets up to run, stumbles, falls . . .

The Horseman strides after . . .

Up the field, Ichabod gets to his knees, feeling his chest with both hands, not quite understanding, struggling to shake off delirium . . .

> **YOUNG MASBATH**
> Sir, you're . . . you're not dead . . .

> **ICHABOD**
> Not . . . yet . . .

Ichabod looks up, trying to comprehend . . .

Lady Van Tassel had turned her horse, her back to us, keeping her distance from the Horseman. Beyond her, Katrina flees this direction with the Horseman at her heels.

Ichabod's focused on something . . .

The black **SADDLEBAG** slung over Lady Van Tassel's horse.

Ichabod rises out of pure determination, runs . . .

Katrina runs . . . the Horseman is closing on her.

Lady Van Tassel watches, grinning, but at the last second something catches her eye and she turns, just as . . .

Ichabod **LEAPS** . . .

TACKLES Lady Van Tassel off of her horse, taking her down to the ground **HARD** . . . her bag falling open . . .

The Horseman's skull rolling out . . .

Ichabod scrambles toward the skull—but falls, halted. Lady Van Tassel grips his leg, holding him.

Young Masbath grabs a heavy, broken **TREE LIMB** off the ground.

The Horseman is mere yards behind Katrina . . .

Ichabod struggles to get free from Lady Van Tassel, can't break her grip when, **BANG**—Young Masbath **SMASHES** Lady Van Tassel over the head with the tree limb. She's out.

The Horseman catches Katrina . . .

Ichabod scrambles free, running, reaching for the skull . . . grasping it . . .

165

The Horseman holds Katrina ready by her hair as she falls to her knees, screaming and struggling. The Horseman raises his sword . . .

Ichabod rises, **THROWS** the skull with all his might . . .

> ICHABOD (CONT'D)
> Horseman!

The skull spins through the air . . .

The Horseman suddenly drops Katrina, reaches up with one hand . . . catches the skull.

Katrina runs. Ichabod runs to meet her, grabs her as she falls. Together, they back away from the Horseman . . .

The Horseman holds the skull out . . . brings it to his shoulders, to its rightful place. **THUNDER POUNDS.**

TRANSFORMATION begins—blood and flesh rise up from the Horseman's throat and grip the skull . . .

Young Masbath watches in awe.

The Horseman's reformation continues. Muscle forms. Liquids become solids. He is made whole once more, the same evil, human face we saw in Baltus's stories.

The Horseman looks to Ichabod and Katrina, touches his restored face. Daredevil rides up, **SCREECH-ING.** The Horseman replaces his sword, climbs into the saddle.

He rides toward Katrina and Ichabod, but he does not want them. They are so exhausted they fall down. Young Masbath comes to stand with them.

The Horseman leans to grab Lady Van Tassel's unconscious form, pulls her up across Daredevil's back.

The Horseman rides away with her.

Ichabod and Katrina watch him go. They look at each other, then kiss gratefully. Ichabod looks to Young Masbath . . .

> ICHABOD (CONT'D)
> How are you, Young Masbath?

> YOUNG MASBATH
> Weary, sir.

Ichabod holds out his arm. Masbath comes over. They embrace. Katrina touches the burned bullet hole in Ichabod's clothing.

> KATRINA
> I thought I had lost you.

Ichabod reaches into his clothing, takes out a **BOOK** he kept in an inner pocket close to his heart . . .

The *BOOK OF SPELLS* with a bullet lodged in it.

Katrina wraps her arms around Ichabod.

220 EXT. WESTERN WOODS, TREE OF THE DEAD—NIGHT

HOOFBEATS.

The Horseman enters the clearing, holding on to Lady Van Tassel. Ahead, the Tree of the Dead awaits.

Lady Van Tassel is awakening . . .

The Horseman grips Lady Van Tassel's hair, pulling her face up
closer to his, just as she opens her eyes . . .

Lady Van Tassel screams . . .

As the Horseman brings his face to meet hers, about to engage in a **KISS**, his jagged teeth open wide.

Ahead, the twisted tree's wound opens, deep and glowing, as Daredevil picks up speed . . .

221 EXT. WESTERN WOODS, TREE OF THE DEAD—NIGHT

Daredevil **JUMPS** in the air just as a **LIGHTNING BOLT** blasts down from the sky, striking the Horseman . . .

For an instant, Horseman and horse are transformed, **SKELETONS OF LIGHT**, entering the tree!

Silence and smoke.

At the tree, Lady Van Tassel's hand sticks out from the tight-shut suture.

The sewn wound on her palm seeps blood as her fingers curl.

222 EXT. NEW YORK CITY STREET, ICHABOD'S HOME—DAY

A coach pulls up to Ichabod's home. Ichabod is the driver.

He gets off, goes and opens the coach door. He helps Katrina down. Next, Young Masbath sticks his head out.

Katrina holds Young Masbath's hand. Ichabod comes to hold Katrina's hand.

A **STRAY CAT** watches them—

Young Masbath looks entranced at the **BUSTLING METROPOLIS**.

YOUNG MASBATH

Oh, my!

KATRINA

(equally impressed)
And cobbled streets!

ICHABOD

(proudly)

Yes . . . New York, New York! Just in time for the new century! It's
the modern age, Katrina!

KATRINA

It's always the modern age, Ichabod . . . but the ancient ones endure.

Large snowflakes begin to fall upon the scene.

Ichabod puts an arm around Katrina and the other arm around Masbath.

The **CAT** is black with one white paw . . . the Cat from Ichabod's dreams . . . The **CAT** turns to look at
the trio.

BCU—The **CAT'S EYES ARE HUMAN, INTELLIGENT, KINDLY** . . . They are Ichabod's Mother's eyes.

Ichabod, Katrina and Young Masbath enter Ichabod's house, as the **SNOW** continues to fall.

THE END

PARAMOUNT PICTURES AND MANDALAY PICTURES PRESENT A SCOTT RUDIN/AMERICAN ZOETROPE PRODUCTION
A TIM BURTON FILM JOHNNY DEPP CHRISTINA RICCI "SLEEPY HOLLOW" MIRANDA RICHARDSON MICHAEL GAMBON
CASPER VAN DIEN JEFFREY JONES MUSIC BY DANNY ELFMAN COSTUME DESIGNER COLLEEN ATWOOD PRODUCTION DESIGNER RICK HEINRICHS EDITED BY CHRIS LEBENZON
DIRECTOR OF PHOTOGRAPHY EMMANUEL LUBEZKI CO-PRODUCER KEVIN YAGHER EXECUTIVE PRODUCERS FRANCIS FORD COPPOLA LARRY FRANCO BASED UPON THE STORY BY WASHINGTON IRVING
SCREEN STORY BY KEVIN YAGHER AND ANDREW KEVIN WALKER SCREENPLAY BY ANDREW KEVIN WALKER PRODUCED BY SCOTT RUDIN ADAM SCHROEDER

www.sleepyhollowmovie.com DOLBY DIGITAL IN SELECTED THEATRES DIRECTED BY TIM BURTON READ THE POCKET BOOK © 1999 BY PARAMOUNT PICTURES AND MANDALAY PICTURES LLC. ALL RIGHTS RESERVED.